T0266614

BBC

DOCTOR WHO

TARDIS
TYPE 40

INSTRUCTION MANUAL

BBC
DOCTOR WHO

TARDIS
TYPE 40

INSTRUCTION MANUAL

WRITTEN BY
RICHARD ATKINSON AND MIKE TUCKER

ILLUSTRATIONS BY
GAVIN RYMILL

BBC
BOOKS

CONTENTS

TARDIS
REGISTRATION CERTIFICATE

MODEL	Type 40 / Mark III TT capsule ('The TARDIS')
PLANET OF ORIGIN	Gallifrey – spatial co-ordinates 10-0-11-0-0 by 0-2 from Galactic Zero Centre
DATE OF REGISTRATION:	20/01/309903
PERSONNEL:	"The Doctor" (and various associates)

NOTES: This space-time capsule is registered as the responsibility of the Doctor (formerly of the Prydonian chapter) on the occasion of his official pardon, following his exile to the planet Earth. The Doctor has changed his/her appearance many times (see attached image data).

THE FIRST DOCTOR stole this capsule from the repair bay and, disabling the recall circuits, evaded the Time Lords for quite some time.

THE SECOND DOCTOR was eventually apprehended and put on trial.

THE THIRD DOCTOR was exiled to Earth, the secret of the TARDIS taken from him. He was eventually pardoned and granted permission to continue his travels.

UPDATES:

THE FOURTH DOCTOR temporarily became President of the High Council of Time Lords.

THE FIFTH DOCTOR was also appointed President, following the disqualification of President Borusa.

THE SIXTH DOCTOR later learned that having wilfully neglected the responsibility of that great office, he had been deposed.

THE SEVENTH DOCTOR continued his travels in the TARDIS, during which time details of his mysterious past came to light – suggesting links to Time Lord prehistory.

This TARDIS was recalled at the outbreak of the Time War, but while **THE EIGHTH DOCTOR** helped people where he could, he refused to fight.

'THE WAR DOCTOR' – Owing to an identity crisis, the Doctor refuses to acknowledge the time he spent fighting in the Great Time War.

THE NINTH DOCTOR carried on travelling in the belief that he destroyed Gallifrey and the Time Lords to end the war, and that this TARDIS was the last of its kind.

THE TENTH DOCTOR and **THE ELEVENTH DOCTOR** along with their other incarnations retroactively used this TARDIS to save Gallifrey at the point it might otherwise have been destroyed.

THE TWELFTH DOCTOR returned to Gallifrey and sent the President and High Council into exile for their activities during the Time War.

THE THIRTEENTH DOCTOR – The current primary operator of this TARDIS.

THE FIRST
DOCTOR

THE SECOND
DOCTOR

THE THIRD
DOCTOR

THE FOURTH
DOCTOR

THE FIFTH
DOCTOR

THE SIXTH
DOCTOR

THE SEVENTH
DOCTOR

THE EIGHTH
DOCTOR

THE WAR
DOCTOR

THE NINTH
DOCTOR

THE TENTH
DOCTOR

THE ELEVENTH
DOCTOR

THE TWELFTH
DOCTOR

THE THIRTEENTH DOCTOR

TARDIS USER MANUAL

WELCOME

This manual is designed to furnish a qualified operator with a summary of all the primary functions of the Type 40 travel capsule (hereafter referred to as the TARDIS). In theory, this craft can take its occupants to any point in time and space. In practice, there are some limits of which owners should take note.

For your convenience, when materialising, the TARDIS tends towards a very narrow range of spatial locations: the surface of a planet, inside a building, space vessel or natural enclosed area. Overriding the navigational systems could result in the TARDIS dangling in mid-air over the sea (fig 0.01), or materialising on a cloud (fig 0.02). Temporally, the TARDIS will become unstable as it approaches the origin of space-time – the event known as the Big Bang. Equally, as the cosmos disperses at the end of the universe it will become impossible to plot a stable course.

A number of space-time co-ordinates are prohibited for various reasons. Some points have been declared off limits as moments of intergalactic special interest. There are pivotal moments that are key to maintaining the integrity of the web of time. Naturally, there are many perilous situations throughout all time that any prudent traveller will want to avoid.

Owing to its unique relationship with time, the TARDIS will be considered both an "antiquated piece of junk" and "the most powerful ship in the universe" and all summations in between. In truth, this is a standard model – neither as basic nor as advanced as other TARDISes – but with regular servicing and routine modifications it should remain in operation for many aeons.

Fig 0.01

Fig 0.02

Fig 0.01 and **0.02.**
Incorrect application of the navigation systems

Fig 0.03. Signage on the front of the TARDIS.

THE MANUAL

- Using psychic printing techniques, this user's guide will – like the TARDIS itself – be presented to you in your native or chosen language (fig 0.03).

- The manual is synced with your TARDIS's core systems, which means specific observations can be made about the continued operation (and non-operation) of this capsule. It should remain updated (if it stops syncing consult the publishers for the possibility of a second edition).

Fig 0.03

■ Any wording on the exterior of the TARDIS will be presented to you in your native language

POLICE TELEPHONE

FREE FOR
USE OF PUBLIC

ADVICE & ASSISTANCE
OBTAINABLE IMMEDIATELY

OFFICERS & CARS
RESPOND TO
URGENT CALLS

PULL TO OPEN

■ This sign is sometimes translated using the phrase "urgent calls" and sometimes "all calls"

■ Although the phrase "Pull to Open" refers to the small cupboard this panel is attached to, even the TARDIS itself thinks it is strange to have the word 'pull' printed on a door that you open by pushing

CASE STUDIES

The case studies contained within this manual are drawn from real-world events from the relative timeline of this TARDIS Type 40 TT Capsule.

Where possible the events presented have taken place directly within the capsule's experiential collection range; however, there are occasions where supplemental information has been obtained from TARDIS memory nodes, collected directly from the minds of crewmembers via the telepathic circuits.

Although operators are expected to abide by the Time Lords' strict non-intervention policy, the Academy is aware that circumstances can arise where interaction with alien affairs is unavoidable. Therefore it is recommended that TARDIS operators read these case studies relating to the Doctor carefully, as they provide important information regarding extreme situations and possible solutions to those situations should they arise.

Space/time co-ordinates for each of these events are indexed according to each planet's relative timeline.

NB: Some of the space/time events concerning the Doctor are restricted under Article 57 of the Shadow Proclamation (Subsection 12: Jurisdiction of the Celestial Intervention Agency). Viewing of these data extracts may require additional security clearance. Please contact your appointed Castellan's office if you require access to these files. Where appropriate we have provided alternative reference examples for non-classified works that can be accessed without security clearance. All of these titles are available from the Panopticon Archive with a valid library card (fines will be levied if books are kept out longer than their standard one-hundred-and-fifty year loan period).

CONSTRUCTION

The Time Lord Academy offers seminars and courses that cover the intricacies of temporal engineering: the theory behind space-time travel, problems in dimensional science and the practical steps in constructing a vessel such as the TARDIS.

This user's handbook offers a more representational overview of this subject. Expert knowledge is not vital for the operation of this craft, but even an unskilled amateur should have a broad understanding of the basics, in order to address the concerns of non-Time Lord personnel who may be encountered on the TARDIS's missions.

GROWTH CYCLE

A useful metaphor, when explaining how TARDISes are built, is to say that they are grown rather than constructed. This is true to the extent that the extra-dimensional architecture is extruded from an infinitesimally small space-time event that is grown in accordance with theories of temporal probability. There is, however, a small degree of both virtual and manual construction work that takes place once a TARDIS has been 'born'. Often students from the Academy will be offered placements to oversee the fitting of auxiliary functions, such as the time-path detector, which requires alignment with non-Time Lord technology that might track and pursue the TARDIS (fig 1.01).

Fig 1.01. The time-path detector

Fig 1.02. Access to the Eye of Harmony deep beneath the Panopticon Vaults on Gallifrey.

Fig 1.03. Susan came up with the word TARDIS from the initials: Time And Relative Dimension In Space.

Fig 1.03

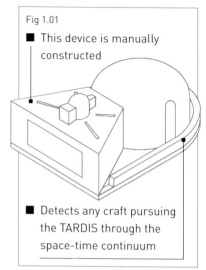

Fig 1.01

■ This device is manually constructed

■ Detects any craft pursuing the TARDIS through the space-time continuum

DATA RETRIEVAL

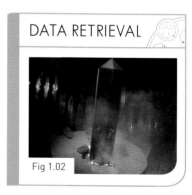

Fig 1.02

The central component of any TARDIS is the Eye of Harmony, which acts as its primary source of power. The Eye is a black hole buried deep beneath the surface of the Time Lord's home planet, Gallifrey (fig 1.02). The awesome forces produced by this collapsed star are stabilised in an eternally dynamic equation against the mass of the planet.

DEFAULT SETTINGS

■ The default exterior setting for the Type 40 TARDIS is a cylindrical structure with a sliding door that is tall enough and wide enough to permit the ingress and egress of High Council officials – and other ranking Time Lords – in the ceremonial robes

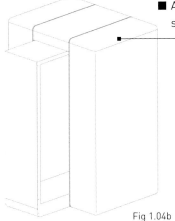

■ Alternative default settings are also used

■ The default interior will be detailed in full in Section V – The Desktop Theme

Fig 1.04a   Fig 1.04b

NAMING

The official designation of this craft is the Type 40 TT Capsule. Informally, however, all Gallifreyan TT capsules are known as TARDISes. Unusually perhaps, the prevalence of this term owes a lot to off-world influences.

The word 'TARDIS' was coined by a Gallifreyan called Susan (fig 1.03), who was one of the original travellers aboard the specific capsule with which this manual is paired. She was the granddaughter of its primary operator, the Doctor. 'TARDIS' or 'the TARDIS' soon became the accepted name for this craft and because it is, without any doubt, the most widely travelled TT capsule, the word has been propagated throughout time and space.

When other TT capsules travel off world they are sometimes recognised as TARDISes, and so the name has fallen into common usage, even on Gallifrey. There are, admittedly, other names for the TT capsules that are used, but if you are not Gallifreyan the TARDIS's translation system [see Section VIII – Telepathic Circuits] will almost certainly render any of these alternatives as 'TARDIS' – as that word is the most likely to be understood in your native language.

The word is made up from initials that stand for Time And Relative Dimension In Space. This acronym reflects the vessel's time travelling capacity and the additional dimensions inside (the plural 'Dimensions' is also sometimes used when explaining what the word stands for).

ARTRON ENERGY

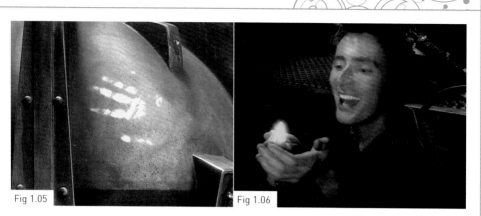

Fig 1.05

Fig 1.06

The Eye of Harmony generates the artron energy that is needed to propel the TARDIS through the space-time vortex. Artron energy is used by a variety of Time Lord devices, as there are relatively few ways that this power can be tapped by external influences, although it can be affected by extremely dense magnetic fields. The Eye itself, in fuelling the TARDIS, generates a high level of background radiation that is absorbed by anyone who sets foot inside. It is mostly harmless and, in rare cases, this absorbed artron energy can be drawn upon to jump-start dormant technology (fig 1.05).

Time Lords who have high levels of artron energy are particularly resilient to psychic attacks and can, in exceptional circumstances, use these reserves to convert their life force into energy that can be used as a power source (fig 1.06).

Fig 1.05. Residual artron energy triggering re-activation of a Gallifreyan containment unit, also known as the Genesis Ark (see Section XI – Modifications).

Fig 1.06. The life force of a Time Lord can be used to power an emergency reboot of the TARDIS primary systems.

All TARDISes have a trans-dimensional link to the Eye of Harmony and rely on it as an inexhaustible supply of energy. If the link between the TARDIS and the Eye is severed, operations will be severely limited to stored power reserves, or any alternative compatible power sources that can be found. The TARDIS can, for example, refuel by materialising near a rift in time and space. It's a drastic measure, but the life force of a Time Lord can be used to jump start the TARDIS systems in such an emergency (see box out: Artron Energy).

The vast power of the Eye itself can also be harnessed in crystalline form (known as a subset of the Eye of Harmony – fig 1.07) and used to punch holes through reality itself.

Accepting that a collapsed star dwells at the heart of the TARDIS, a novice might quite reasonably wonder how you can contain such a gigantic elemental force in something the size of a small cupboard. The TARDIS, of course, is dimensionally transcendental, which means it can contain an enormous inner space within a much, much smaller exterior.

INSIDE THE BOX

This key Time Lord discovery can be expressed in very simple terms. Imagine two cubes of equal size. If you held one in your hand and viewed the other from a distance, the second cube would appear smaller than the first. If you could keep it that distance away, and yet also have it in your hand, this 'smaller' cube would fit inside the 'larger' one. This analogy might help others understand that the interior of the TARDIS is literally inside the exterior. When entering, the occupants are not spirited to another realm. They are not squeezed or squashed relative to normal space. The inside of a TARDIS simply contains additional dimensions that make it possible to accommodate bigger spaces inside smaller ones. If you shake the outside of the TARDIS, or tilt it, the effect will be transferred within, unless the relative gravity settings have been calibrated to nullify such turbulence.

Many functions such as this will be integrated into the day-to-day running of this machine. This is managed by the TARDIS's central systems, which during the assembly process manifest themselves as a sentient intelligence. This is the consequence of the manner in which its complex systems are integrated, augmented by its ability to gather data from all of time and space.

It should be noted, however, that unqualified tampering, *ad hoc* adjustments and modifications are likely to introduce glitches and impede smooth running. A notable example of a systems breakdown such as this is covered in the following chapter.

Shortly after construction, when this TARDIS was first required to deviate from its default settings, it became clear that the chameleon circuit had not been properly 'run in' – the shape it adopted was often not in keeping with the environment in which it had landed, and it had a tendency to stick, remaining in the same form for some time. Because of this, and a number of other serious faults, it was consigned to the repair shop for maintenance. The relevant sections of this manual have been updated in real time to explain in some depth how this issue has persisted over the lifetime of this TARDIS...

■ A crystal from Metebelis III

■ This device, also known as a psychochronograph, amplifies natural psychic abilities

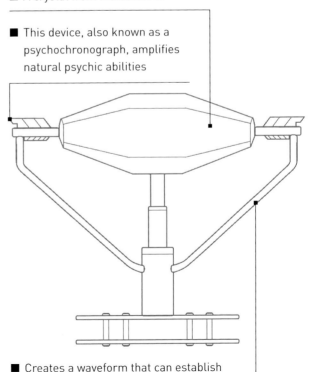

Fig 1.07. A subset of the Eye of Harmony.

■ Creates a waveform that can establish a link between alternate universes

THE OUTER PLASMIC SHELL

Each time this TARDIS materialises in a new location, within the first nanosecond of it landing, it analyses its surroundings, calculates a 12-dimensional data map of everything within a thousand-mile radius, and determines which outer shell would blend in best with its environment, and then it disguises itself as a police telephone box (*fig 2.03*).

This outer plasmic shell, as it is known, is driven by the chameleon circuit (also referred to as the camouflage unit, the electronic chameleon system and, colloquially, as a 'cloaking device'). When it's working properly, a TARDIS can disguise itself as something that would normally be seen in the immediate vicinity, allowing Time Lord field agents to conduct studies of other times and places with minimal chance of

interfering in the established pattern of history.

Simple stone structures such as columns, sarcophagi and pyramids (*fig 2.01*) often blend into the landscape easily (although, a giant pyramid appearing suddenly overnight, out of nowhere, is likely to draw people's attention). One way to avoid the natives of a planet you're visiting noticing something that wasn't previously there, is for your TARDIS to disguise itself as an alternative mode of transport that could have been parked where you land. TARDISes have been known to adopt the shape of vehicles such as buses and aeroplanes (*fig 2.02*). (And by modelling the plasmic shell on a flying vessel, you can to some extent get around the limitations on piloting the outer shell in normal space – see Section IV –

Fig 2.01. Punch a few buttons and the TARDIS becomes a pyramid – or so the theory goes.

Fig 2.02. Another TARDIS, disguised as a Terran aircraft, Concorde.

Fig 2.03. The current appearance of this TARDIS.

DATA RETRIEVAL

Fig 2.01

Fig 2.02

Fig 2.03

Fig 2.04

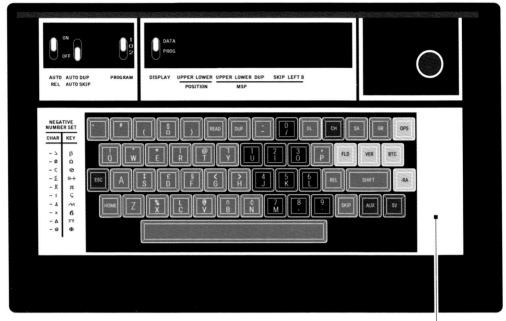

■ This keyboard can be used to manually alter the shape of the TARDIS exterior.

The TARDIS Engines: Case Studies). The shape that is chosen should, at least, provide space for a reasonably sized door – you've got to get in and out.

As indicated above, the TARDIS itself should be capable of selecting an appropriate exterior. The Type 40 model, however, also offers a control panel where a custom design can be programmed in using machine code (fig 2.04).

WARNING
Unfortunately, this TARDIS's chameleon circuit has a persistent fault that has caused it to consolidate in incongruous forms. Early on, it travelled to the planet Earth's 'Twentieth Century' where it first manifested as a police telephone box (full schematics follow on page 21 – fig 2.12), and although this disguise

wasn't completely out-of-step with the surroundings, it was far from being the optimal cover for the TARDIS. Police boxes were usually seen on the corner of the street and it had arrived in a junkyard (see box out: Outer Shell Template).

It was at this point that the chameleon circuit jammed, causing this TARDIS to adopt the form of a police box on a permanent basis. Over the many centuries since, it has remained in this form with only minor changes (further details follow on pages 22 and 23 – fig 2.13). The gradual collapse of non-essential quasi-neural pathways within the system has resulted in the outer shell degrading – often giving it a 'battered' appearance. Conversely, periodic software patches have updated both various design details and the specific shade of blue on its

Fig 2.04. Chameleon circuit controls.

surface (see page 23 – fig 2.14). In addition the continued interaction between the plasmic shell and the machine's much more expansive interior dimensions has caused the TARDIS to fractionally increase in size over time (fig 2.05).

A similar process occurs when the TARDIS reaches the end of its functional lifespan, when a dimensional leak will cause the plasmic shell to expand to towering proportions (see Section XI – Modifications: Case Studies).

It is possible to repair the chameleon circuit using block transfer computations – a way of modelling space-time events through pure calculation. To do this, however, accurate measurements need to be taken from the original object, or objects, sampled by the chameleon circuit.

To date, however, the TARDIS remains stuck as a police box. It has been observed

that perhaps this is a fitting external appearance that suits the craft and its operator. Over the many centuries that the various incarnations of the Doctor have piloted the TARDIS they have frequently offered assistance to those in need, policing time and space. Without being asked, the TARDIS has often taken them where they were needed, and it's even possible that it has chosen to remain as a police box, impeding a number of attempts to rectify the situation.

Fig 2.05

Fig 2.05. The relative sizes of the police box shell over time.

Fig 2.06. The TARDIS adopts the appearance of a police telephone box for the first time.

OUTER SHELL TEMPLATE

The TARDIS's outer shell is based on a type of kiosk, used to house communication devices for local authorities. They were commonplace in the United Kingdom (or UK) region of mid-twentieth century Earth — a planet that this craft has been repeatedly drawn to, owing to the intriguing and often calamitous fortunes of its indigenous people. The police box was first duplicated by the TARDIS when it landed in the UK capital city London in summer 1963 (using the local dating system). The design originates three and a half decades earlier and was the work of Earth architect Gilbert Mackenzie Trench (although, paradoxically, there are rumours he may have been inspired by seeing the TARDIS on one of its trips to the 1920s). Owing to factors in its immediate proximity, however, the TARDIS didn't copy the Trench template precisely. The TARDIS's version of the police box was slightly smaller so it could fit into the cramped conditions of the junkyard in which it materialised (fig 2.06).

Fig 2.06

DATA RETRIEVAL

Fig 2.07

Fig 2.08

Fig 2.09

■ Paint applied to the outer shell will be absorbed into the three-dimensional matrix (*fig 2.07*) and, if the chameleon circuits don't trigger a change, then the modifications will remain when the TARDIS rematerialises. If the paintwork is a thin, brittle layer it may flake off as the TARDIS dematerialises (*fig 2.08*). Objects embedded in the outer layer of the TARDIS's skin will be preserved in transit through the space-time vortex (*fig 2.09*). Materials affixed to the shell that combust at low temperatures, however, may burn.

■ The artefact on which this TARDIS shell is modelled includes a cupboard with a telephone – used to contact the authorities. For most of this craft's operational lifespan, it was disconnected and served no purpose. For a period, however, it was wired up to the TARDIS's own communication systems and would ring if anyone contacted the TARDIS.

THE INNER PLASMIC SHELL

By default the outer plasmic shell is isolated from the main control room by a set of internal doors (fig 2.10). However: some of the remodelled versions of the control room (see Section V – The Desktop Theme) include the reverse of the exterior shell on the inside.

■ These doors are operated remotely from the control console

■ The doors can be opened manually using a crank inserted here

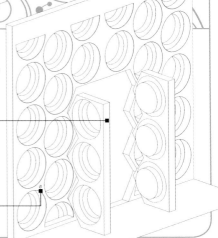
Fig 2.10

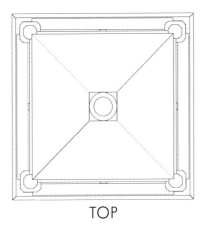

TOP

Fig 2.11

Fig 2.11. Icons on the outer shell generated based on local data collection.

Fig 2.12. The orignal proportions of the TARDIS when it first assumed the shape of a police telephone box.

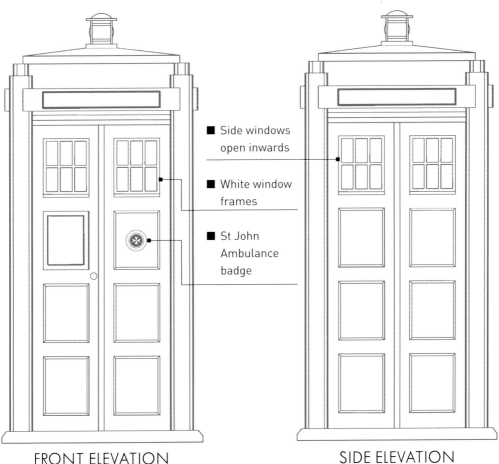

■ Side windows open inwards

■ White window frames

■ St John Ambulance badge

FRONT ELEVATION

SIDE ELEVATION

Fig 2.12

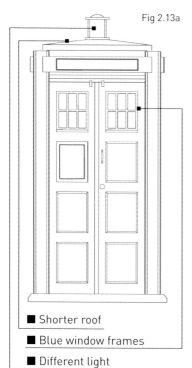

Fig 2.13a

- Shorter roof
- Blue window frames
- Different light
- No St John Ambulance badge

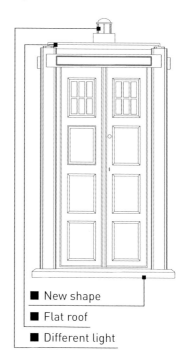

Fig 2.13b

- New shape
- Flat roof
- Different light

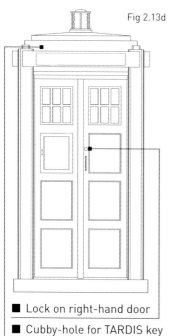

Fig 2.13d

- Lock on right-hand door
- Cubby-hole for TARDIS key

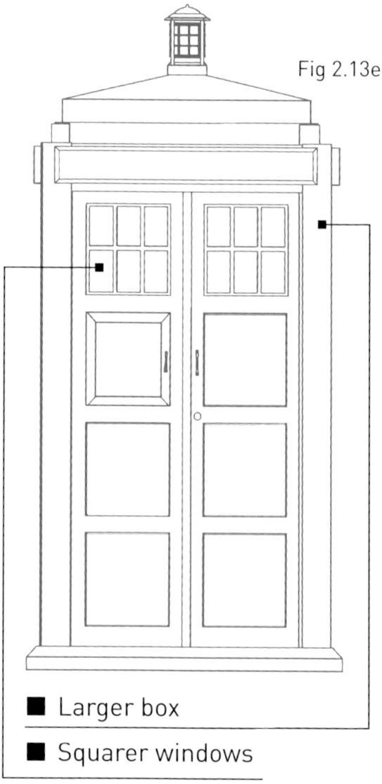

Fig 2.13e

- Larger box
- Squarer windows

Fig 2.13c

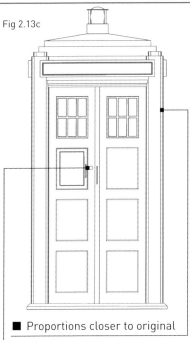

- ■ Proportions closer to original
- ■ New position for lock

Fig 2.14

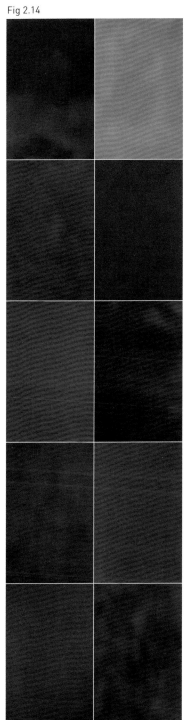

Fig 2.13f

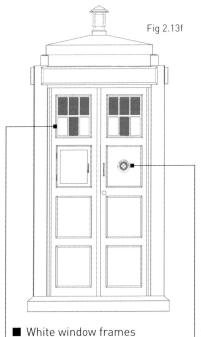

- ■ White window frames
- ■ New St John Ambulance badge

Fig 2.13. Variations on the police box shell over the centuries.

Fig 2.14. Range of colours used on the TARDIS shell.

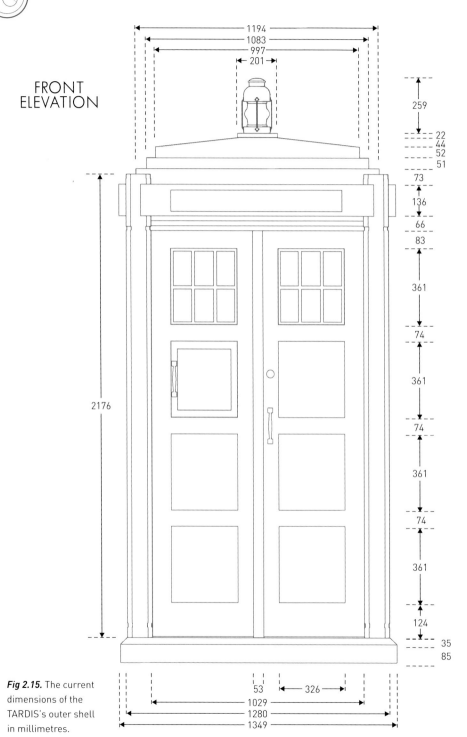

FRONT
ELEVATION

1194
1083
997
201

259
22
44
52
51
73
136
66
83
361
74
361
74
361
74
361
124
35
85

2176

53
326
1029
1280
1349

Fig 2.15. The current
dimensions of the
TARDIS's outer shell
in millimetres.

WINDOW

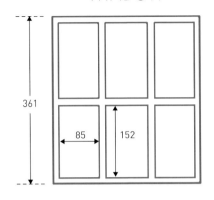

361

85

152

TOP

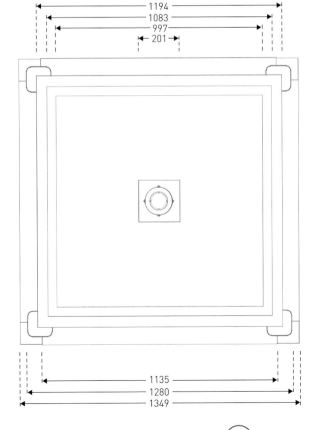

1194
1083
997
201

1135
1280
1349

SIDE ELEVATION

CASE STUDY

THE CRYON INCIDENT

TELEPATHIC CIRCUIT MEMORY NODE RETRIEVAL
NODE: 6T/138
SPATIAL CO-ORDINATES: Earth (Terra) / Telos.
TEMPORAL CO-ORDINATES: Local Dateline: 20th Century.
TARDIS CREW: The Sixth Doctor (Gallifreyan), Perpugilliam
Brown (Terran).

NOTES:

At the point that the Doctor 'appropriated' this TARDIS from Gallifrey, it was in dry dock for repairs, primarily because of faults to the guidance systems, but also because of an error that had developed in the chameleon circuit.

Shortly after fleeing Gallifrey, the Doctor and his granddaughter Susan landed on the planet Earth in the Twentieth Century segment of that planet's timeline. Upon landing, the chameleon circuit finally failed entirely, resulting in the outer plasmic shell sticking in the form of a primitive communications device known as a 'police box' (see Page 19: Outer Shell Template).

Despite the incongruous nature of its appearance, the TARDIS remained in this form until, due to instability caused by trauma during his fifth regeneration, the Doctor attempted to make repairs to the chameleon circuit himself without adhering to recommended service procedure.

Whist the Doctor's repairs did result in a temporary restoration of function, the haphazard nature of those repairs made the circuit behave in an erratic manner, causing the TARDIS to materialise using a variety of templates, none of which were pertinent to the surroundings in which the capsule materialised.

This problem manifested itself both on Earth and on the planet Telos (see visual files attached).

There are several problems inherent in making these kinds of unauthorised repairs without proper care, the most obvious being that it becomes virtually impossible to locate the entry point to a capsule if the parameters for the entry/exit points have not been set in advance of materialisation. It can also result in the capsule being too large for its target destination, resulting in localised damage to the materialisation site.

The inability for any TARDIS to adequately disguise its true nature also exposes the operators to intrusion. In the brief span of this particular space/time event, unauthorised entry was gained to the TARDIS by no less than three different alien species; TARDIS operators are reminded of their security obligations when landing on a planet at level five or lower.

Because of the unsatisfactory nature of the Doctor's repairs, the circuit finally failed again during its final journey on the planet Telos, defaulting the outer plasmic shell to its last stable configuration — that of a police box.

ADDITIONAL:

During this space/time event, the Doctor discovered that the Cybermen had acquired access to a time vessel and had set in motion plans to alter the timeline of the planet Earth by preventing the destruction of the planet Mondas.

(For further information please refer to relevant historical documentation regarding the History of the Cybermen — several comprehensive histories are contained within the Panopticon Archives.)

Fortunately the Cyber-race's unfamiliarity with temporal technology, coupled with timely intervention by the Celestial Intervention Agency in subtly directing the Doctor to become involved, meant that this attempt ended in failure and no significant damage to the timeline took place.

Nonetheless, Time Lords are instructed to ensure that any encounter with the Cyber-race, where evidence exists that they are using temporal technology, should be reported to the CIA immediately. Direct intervention such as that taken by the Doctor should not be attempted other than by authorised temporal agents.

THE TARDIS KEY

Using a simple key to gain access to one of the most sophisticated vessels ever created might seem archaic. The TARDIS key, however, is itself a very advanced piece of technology with a variety of uses.

The key maintains a direct link with the TARDIS at all times. Even if the TARDIS is isolated by a temporal disturbance the key should be able to summon it back (see Case Study, page 32). Conversely, the TARDIS can be concealed, a second out of sync with your current time zone, using the key as an anchor.

The TARDIS can send messages using the key – making it glow (fig 3.01) to alert the crew of an activity that needs their attention. Time Lords can even use the key to gain access to TARDISes other than their own. Without the key, you will need a Type 40 cypher ident key to cancel the double curtain trimonic barrier.

KEY DIFFERENCES

The key can take on various guises. This isn't the same technology that is used to disguise the TARDIS's outer plasmic shell, however. Instead, the key uses a perception filter that makes anyone observing the key see it in a certain way. In the case of the TARDIS paired with this manual, most people see the type of key that would fit the lock on a police box, but this isn't always the case. A perception filter can be psychically influenced. While exiled on Earth by the Time Lords, the Doctor willed his key to adopt a more elegant shape (fig 3.04), and he often wore it on a chain around his neck. The key has taken on a number of other guises, including one that featured a symbol used by ranking Time Lords, known as the Seal of Rassilon (fig 3.05).

The perception filter also ensures that anyone using the key sees a keyhole on the TARDIS that matches the key (fig 3.02). It also has other uses, and can be adapted so the key makes anyone wearing it imperceptible to others.

Even though the key is very difficult to destroy – it is only adversely affected by

Fig 3.01. A signal from the TARDIS.

Fig 3.02. The Doctor's spare key.

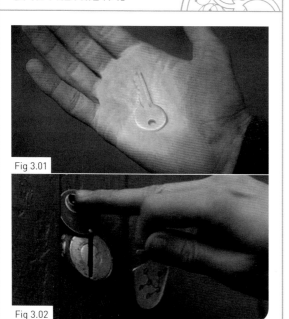

DATA RETRIEVAL

Fig 3.01

Fig 3.02

THE TARDIS LOCK

The TARDIS lock can be configured in various different ways to ensure that only authorised personnel have access. One simple method, adopted when the Type 40 was quite new, was for the inside of the lock to contain 21 positions — only one of which would open the door.

A slightly more complex process was to use a metabolism detector. Providing it was set, only a Time Lord would be able to open the doors.

The doors can be locked from the inside, so that they key won't work for anyone. When using the default desktop theme (see Section V — The Desktop Theme), the doors are locked from the console, but if the outer plasmic shell has its own functional lock with a snib, then flicking that will engage the central locking mechanism.

Careful maintenance of the lock and associated shielding is advised. Some alien races have technology that, in rare circumstances, can remove the lock (fig 3.03). Certain focused rays can also freeze the lock mechanism. This action can be reversed by refracting a specific range of ultraviolet radiation through a type of gemstone that has its own special properties.

Fig 3.03

Fig 3.04

extreme temperatures — the Doctor has made numerous copies, some of which he has distributed among his travelling companions. Following a situation where his key was taken from him, the Doctor also stored a spare key in a secret compartment above the TARDIS door.

The key can be modified so that it can be used to lock the doors from a distance. A combination of this remote locking mechanism and the special affinity that the Doctor has developed with the TARDIS over the years, means the door can now be opened and closed with a click of the fingers.

Fig 3.05

Fig 3.03. The TARDIS lock is stolen.

Fig 3.04. The Doctor's own design for the key.

Fig 3.05. A version of the key carrying a symbol of the Doctor's Time Lord credentials.

THE REAPER INCIDENT

TELEPATHIC CIRCUIT MEMORY NODE RETRIEVAL
NODE: 1/27:8
SPATIAL CO-ORDINATES: Earth (Terra).
TEMPORAL CO-ORDINATES: Local Dateline: 21st Century.
TARDIS CREW: The Ninth Doctor (Gallifreyan), Rose Tyler (Terran).

NOTES:
Whilst Gallifreyan time travellers are well aware of their duties and obligations with regard to the Laws of Time, there are dangers inherent in giving other, less responsible, species access to time travel technology.

Whilst the Doctor himself is prone to interfere in a way that pushes the boundaries of acceptable Time Lord behaviour, it is acknowledged that it is rare that he allows the others who travel with him to do likewise.

On one notable occasion, however, he was persuaded by Rose Tyler (see Index File: Bad Wolf / The Moment) to take her back into her own past in order to witness the moment of her father's death.

Whilst this itself was already a breach of temporal guidelines, the Doctor compounded things still further by making a *second* trip to the same point in time, resulting in multiple versions of himself and Miss Tyler occupying the same point in the space-time continuum.

This temporal conundrum might have gone by without incident, if not for Miss Tyler's direct interference in the fate of her father – Peter Tyler – saving his life and altering his personal timeline at a point where temporal strands were already stretched to breaking point.

The resultant time anomaly caused a fracture in the time vortex, jettisoning the TARDIS interior from this dimension and attracting temporal scavengers known as 'Reapers' — a sub-species of the Chronovores. (Further information can be found in the three volume work 'Creatures of Infinity: Kronos and Other Native Vortex Species' by Transduction Controller Rodan.)

Attempting to rectify the situation, the Doctor attempted to use the telepathic link that exists between a TARDIS and its key in order to try to reformat this capsule within this dimension. Whilst this attempt was in theory possible — and initially appeared to have had partial success — it eventually failed as the Doctor himself fell victim to these creatures following a temporal 'short circuit' caused by Rose Tyler directly interacting with her infant self (see Index File: Blinovitch Limitation Effect). At this point the telepathic connection between the Doctor, the key and the TARDIS was irreversibly severed.

Ultimately, Mr Tyler, showing an uncommon understanding of the workings of temporal mechanics for someone from a level two civilisation, reset the timelines by bringing about his own death in accordance with established history. At this point both the Doctor and this TARDIS were reinstated to their correct point in space/time.

These events serve to illustrate that TARDIS operators have a responsibility to keep the web of time intact, and that there are no excuses for allowing non-Gallifreyans to interfere with established temporal order. Deliberate disregard for these rules can result in a custodial sentence and removal of all time-travel privileges.

Evidence of Chronovore activity outside the confines of the time vortex is an indicator of damage to the space/time continuum and should be reported to a senior Time Lord authority immediately.

THE TARDIS ENGINES

When activated, the engines deconstruct the TARDIS – a process known as dematerialisation – and transfer it intact into the space-time vortex, which acts as a conduit between two discrete space-time co-ordinates. The engines then rematerialise the TARDIS at the other end.

During materialisation the sound of the engines can be heard: a deep, echoing sound, like a thunderous grinding of gears, that rises and falls as the TARDIS is ripped out of – or forced into – normal space. It may sound like the TARDIS is being landed with the brakes on, but this is perfectly normal and all capsules make this sound when they take off and land. If deemed necessary for a stealthy arrival, however, careful calibration can minimise this noise, or even eliminate it entirely.

The TARDIS will fade from view, or gradually solidify. Occasionally, when being piloted by a direct link from Gallifrey it can just instantly disappear and reappear. As it emerges into normal space-time, it displaces the atmosphere it emerges into. This can create a disturbance – and if the engines are not properly maintained then, over time, the disruption a materialisation causes will become more dramatic.

Rather than displacing the volume that the TARDIS emerges into, that space can be relocated within the control room. This can be useful to isolate a threat that needs to be neutralised, rescue people

Fig 4.01. A mark I dematerialisation circuit.

from a dangerous situation, or to transfer heavy objects into the TARDIS.

VITAL CIRCUITS

It is worth keeping a spare dematerialisation circuit (*fig 4.01*) handy, as the TARDIS will be useless without one. A lot of energy is transferred through the circuit and if, for instance, you attempt to dematerialise too close to the event horizon of a black hole you might end up blowing the circuit.

Rather than simply dematerialising and rematerialising the TARDIS, the engines can be used to fly it through normal space. This might be useful if you need to pursue another vehicle (see page 44 – Case Studies) or wish to carry out visual surveillance from the air.

Given enough energy – and this manoeuvre requires extraordinary reserves of power – the engines can also take the TARDIS out of normal space and time and into alternative universes, a procedure that this craft has executed several times.

It should be noted that although the engines are capable of moving the TARDIS between alternate planes of reality, in addition to the attendant dangers, it is not part of the ship's intended operational parameters. Anyone embarking on such a journey runs the risk of not being able to return to normal space. At the very least, this activity is likely to result in permanent damage to the core systems.

THE SPACE-TIME VORTEX

The vortex is a domain that exists alongside normal space-time. It's not just the TARDIS that can travel in the vortex — other time-travelling vessels, even entire planets, have been known to travel through it. Such transit, however, is extraordinarily perilous. Most races directly exposed to forces within the vortex will be killed instantly, although Time Lords can survive for a short while.

The vortex manipulator — a wristband that can transport an individual through time — only provides a minimal amount of protection, which is why it is such a dangerous way to travel.

Energy from the vortex is channelled through the heart of the TARDIS — and can be absorbed by anyone looking into it. Again this is likely to result in fatality and will trigger regeneration in a Time Lord.

There is a link between the vortex and the Time Lords' ability to regenerate and, under certain circumstances, children conceived within the vortex can be born with this ability.

Fig 4.01

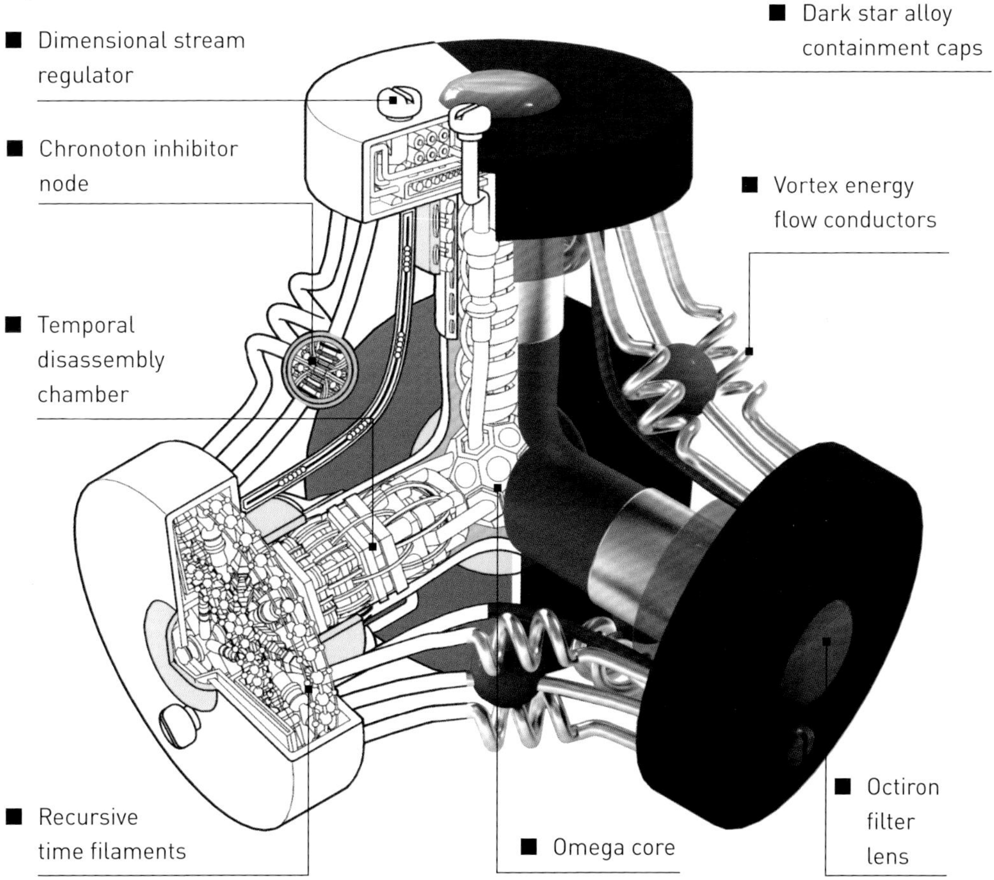

- Dimensional stream regulator

- Chronoton inhibitor node

- Temporal disassembly chamber

- Recursive time filaments

- Dark star alloy containment caps

- Vortex energy flow conductors

- Octiron filter lens

- Omega core

THE TEMPORAL ORBIT INCIDENT

TELEPATHIC CIRCUIT MEMORY NODE RETRIEVAL
NODE: 50/LDX071Y/01X
SPATIAL CO-ORDINATES: San Francisco, Earth (Terra).
TEMPORAL CO-ORDINATES: Local Dateline: 20th / 21st Century.
TARDIS CREW: The Seventh Doctor (Gallifreyan), The Eighth Doctor (Gallifreyan), Grace Holloway (Terran), Chang Lee (Terran), the Master – incarnation indeterminate (Gallifreyan).

NOTES:

All TARDISes are fitted with a trans-dimensional interface linking them back to the Eye of Harmony beneath the Panopticon on Gallifrey. In emergency situations it may be necessary to access that interface for repair or refuelling purposes. In normal circumstances most TARDIS operators will automatically be granted security access to the Eye, but as illustrated below there are significant dangers inherent in leaving that interface open for extended periods.

During the events surrounding the Doctor's regeneration from his seventh body into his eighth, the renegade Time Lord known as the Master gained access to the Eye of Harmony interface of this capsule and caused catastrophic

damage to the timeline of the planet Earth. (Celestial Intervention Agency Files on known Gallifreyan criminals are generally restricted, so TARDIS operators are directed towards the controversial memoir 'Malfeasance: When Time Lords Go Bad' by former Castellan Spandrell.)

Prior to his extermination by the Daleks on Skaro, the Master had requested that in the event of his death, the Doctor should take his remains back to Gallifrey. Whist the Doctor was undertaking this task the Master put into play a complex plan to acquire a new regeneration cycle by appropriating the Doctor's body.

Infecting the TARDIS console using a Deathworm Morphant (See Index File: Flora and Fauna of Skaro / Morgs), the Master forced the ship into a landing on Earth during the last days of that planet's Twentieth Century, and subsequent events resulted in the Doctor's seventh regeneration.

Taking advantage of the Doctor's absence due to an extended bout of regeneration trauma, the Master gained access to the

TARDIS's cloister room interface with the Eye of Harmony. Although initially unsuccessful in his attempts to gain access to the Eye himself, the Master was ultimately able to use the retinal print of a juvenile Terran named Chang Lee to open the interface (see Index File: Gallifreyan Security Systems: Sub File: Archetryx). He then used the temporal faculties of the Eye in order to track down the newly regenerated Doctor and put into motion his attempt to steal his remaining incarnations. This only failed due to the intervention of human cardiologist Doctor Grace Holloway, who died in the process along with Chang Lee.

Leaving the interface open for such an extended period caused significant damage to the localised timestream, and was only rectified by the Doctor using the TARDIS in an unorthodox manner to reset his own timeline. The deaths of Grace Holloway and Chang Lee were also reversed, although there is evidence to support the fact that the TARDIS itself made this decision, rather than the Doctor.

This kind of temporal interference – both in regard to changes to established planetary history, and by using TARDIS energies to reverse terminal situations in primitive biological entities – is not approved.

THE BAD WOLF BAY INCIDENT

TELEPATHIC CIRCUIT MEMORY NODE RETRIEVAL
NODE: 2/28:13
SPATIAL CO-ORDINATES: Earth (Terra) / Alternate Earth.
TEMPORAL CO-ORDINATES: Local Dateline:21st Century.
TARDIS CREW: The Tenth Doctor (Gallifreyan), Rose Tyler (Terran).

NOTES:

TARDIS power systems can occasionally be augmented by additional energy sources to increase power without the inconvenient need to delete internal architecture.

Following an incursion into this universe by an alternate manifestation of the Cyber-Race (see Index File: Parallel Universes) the Doctor's companion Rose Tyler was trapped in a parallel version of Earth with no obvious means of escape. In order to communicate with her one last time the Doctor boosted a holographic projection of himself through a rift in the space-time continuum by channelling energy from a supernova through the TARDIS communications grid.

In emergency situations energy can also be drawn from suitable sources other than the Eye of Harmony. The most suitable form of alternative energy – Rift energy – occurs at either end of breaks in the space/time continuum and can successfully be used to recharge TARDIS power systems. The Doctor has been known to use a rift located in Cardiff, Wales (Terra) on several occasions (see Index File: Torchwood) and has also used Rift energy from bubble universes

(see Section VIII, Case Study 7/33:04, page 112). However recharging in this manner is not recommended unless absolutely necessary, and technical staff request that TARDIS operators use the link to the Eye of Harmony as a first resort to avoid potential problems with incompatible fuel systems that could affect the efficient operation of their capsule.

THE M4 INCIDENT

TELEPATHIC CIRCUIT MEMORY NODE RETRIEVAL
NODE: 3/29:X
SPATIAL CO-ORDINATES: Earth (Terra).
TEMPORAL CO-ORDINATES: Local Dateline: 21st Century.
TARDIS CREW: The Tenth Doctor (Gallifreyan), Donna Noble (Terran).

Type 40 Capsules are primarily trans-dimensional vehicles that operate best within the confines of the space-time continuum, or within a non-gravity environment such as deep space. Whilst all craft are fitted with a 'hover' function, that allow them to occupy a geostationary point within a planet's gravitational field, it is also possible to pilot them in much the same manner as a conventional flying vehicle, although this is not recommended unless the operator is an experienced pilot. (A full list of operators with experience of piloting War TARDISes in atmospheric conditions, or *extremely* experienced operators who flew Bow Ships during the Great War against the Vampires, is available on request.)

For the capsule to operate in this manner, all space/time controls must be set into 'standby'

mode, and the basic hover function engaged. By then selecting the appropriate settings to counter the local gravity of the planet on which the TARDIS is being operated, and reconfiguring the navigational controls to operate as standard 'yaw', 'pitch' and 'roll', the capsule can then be piloted in much the same way as any conventional aircraft.

The Doctor operated this TARDIS in this manner in order to rescue future companion Donna Noble from the robot servants of the Empress of the Racnoss during an attempt by the Empress to revive her race. (There are several historical reference works available relating to the Racnoss and other invasive species from the Old Time within the Panopticon Archive, the most comprehensive being 'Minyans, Spiders and Vampires, Oh My. A Study of Gallifreyan Interference in Established History and its Catastrophic Effects' by former President Pandak III.)

Whilst the Doctor showed considerable skill in piloting the TARDIS solo — particularly given that he was operating the controls remotely whilst leaning out of the open main doors — no care was taken whatsoever with regard to the flight being witnessed by the indigenous population. Indeed, it was observed by several people travelling on the primitive Terran transportation system known as the M4.

If TARDISes are to be flown on planets with grade two status or below, and there is a reasonable expectation of that flight being observed, then operators are requested to set the outer plasmic shell to the form of a contemporary

flying vehicle from that planet. Dimensional patterns for vehicles appropriate to the time period of the planet that you are intending to visit should be downloaded from the TARDIS workshop mainframe prior to leaving Gallifrey.

THE DESKTOP THEME

The primary control room, sometimes referred to as the console room, provides a stark contrast to the TARDIS's outer shell. While the outside is either plain and functional or an otherworldly camouflage, the interior space is a spectacular showcase of Time Lord sophistication (fig 5.01). There are a few vintage touches – mainly seen in the archaic dials, switches, levers and other devices on the control console – that are intended to reflect the vessel's link with history. For the most part, however, this space features a modernist design. The walls are broken up by 'roundels' and hexagonal motifs intended to represent the geometric and circular principles central to theories of space-time travel.

THE EARLY YEARS

The default control room (see pages 50 and 51 – fig 5.06) is a large white space, with heavy double doors. In common with subsequent remodelled control rooms, there is a large six-sided control console in the centre of the room. All of the TARDIS functions can be accessed from here.

Both the control room and the console can be reconfigured, either to make adjustments to the working space or to accommodate minor changes to

Fig 5.01. The original TARDIS interior.

Fig 5.01

the instruments. It would, of course, be impossible to have a dedicated switch for all the TARDIS's many capabilities and so some control panels serve multiple functions. The controls default to certain frequently used functions (further details follow on pages 52 & 53 – fig 5.07), but operators will soon develop their own system for using the controls.

The hexagonal console was designed so that the TARDIS can be operated by a crew of six. Relying on the TARDIS's own intelligent navigation systems it is, of course, possible for an individual to pilot the TARDIS. There are highly complex manoeuvres, however, that require on-the-fly stabilisation and will require a full complement of crewmembers (see Section VII – Force Fields: Case Study – page 106).

Since this TARDIS has been commissioned there have been a number of adjustments to the control area.

The Time Lords grounded the TARDIS for a brief period while the Doctor was in exile for breaking their laws. During this time, the Doctor made a number of ill-conceived attempts to bypass the Time Lords' controls, going as far as dismantling the console and removing it from the TARDIS (fig 5.02).

Bored, during this period of enforced shore leave, the Doctor made the first significant adjustments to what has since become colloquially known as 'the desktop theme' – making some subtle changes to the control panels and introducing a more elaborate

DATA RETRIEVAL

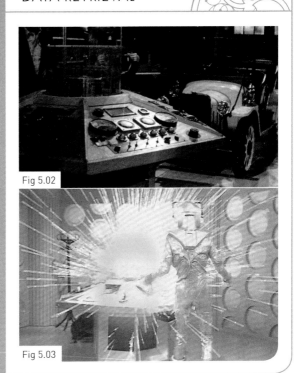

Fig 5.02

Fig 5.03

array of roundels (see pages 54 and 55 – fig 5.08).

The TARDIS soon reverted to a more traditional configuration, however, and remained that way for some time. The Doctor rerouted the 'secondary control room' (see pages 56 and 57 – fig 5.09) to the exterior doors for a short time, while the main control room resolved some temporary glitches and installed some additional cosmetic upgrades (see page 48 – fig 5.04).

Eventually, following damage to the system from an incursion by the Cybermen (fig 5.03), the Doctor decided to give the main control room a proper overhaul. The decorative analogue

Fig 5.02. Outside the box – attempted repairs to the TARDIS console.

Fig 5.03. The Cybermen damage the main control systems.

DATA RETRIEVAL

Fig 5.04a

Fig 5.04b

instrumentation was replaced by a similarly retro 'digital' interface – prominently featuring keyboards and monitors of the early computer age (see pages 62 and 63 – fig 5.17).

To date the TARDIS has archived about 30 different control rooms, a number of which were planned out, but never used (such as the design seen on page 64 – fig 5.18).

More recent variations on the desktop theme have been something of a departure from the futurist design of the default control space. The first of these – featuring a mixture of steel girders, wood panelling and brass fixtures and fittings (see pages 66 and 67 – fig 5.20) – was comprehensively destroyed during the Time War, when a ship the TARDIS had landed on crashed on the planet Karn.

BATTLE TARDIS

The Doctor then remodelled the desktop theme, better to serve his participation in the Time War (see

pages 72 and 73 – fig 5.29). The TARDIS sustained a considerable amount of damage and the Doctor repaired the console with whatever was to hand. After the Time War, he made minimal adjustments, keeping much of the control room as it was as a reminder of the role he'd played in this conflict (see page 74 – fig 5.30).

This version of the TARDIS's control room was damaged when the Tenth Doctor regenerated into the eleventh, and the TARDIS itself redesigned the space. This was a very self-consciously different approach, perhaps chosen to reflect the revised personality of the new Doctor. It was composed mainly of copper and glass, but retained elements that reflected some of the quirkier elements of the previous console (see page 74 – fig 5.31).

Once settled into his new incarnation, the Doctor redecorated the TARDIS reverting to a more traditional design (see page 76 – fig 5.33). Initially it took the form of a functional, futuristic flight deck with a clearly delineated control console (see pages 78 and 79 – fig 5.35). Following yet another regeneration, however, the Doctor filled the space with shelves and clutter and opted for warmer lighting (see page 77 – fig 5.34).

Demonstrating that the Doctor never learns from his mistakes, this control room was again put out of commission when he regenerated on another occasion – necessitating a further new look that persists to this day (see pages 84 and 85 – fig 5.44). More details concerning the current desktop theme can be found on pages 86 and 87.

Fig 5.04. Minor changes to the default control console.

Fig 5.05. Floorplan of the default control room.

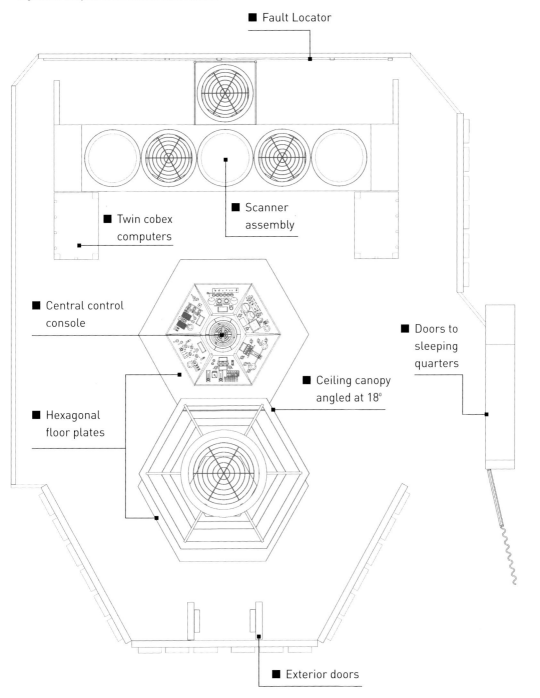

■ Fault Locator

■ Scanner
assembly

■ Twin cobex
computers

■ Central control
console

■ Doors to
sleeping
quarters

■ Ceiling canopy
angled at 18°

■ Hexagonal
floor plates

■ Exterior doors

THE DEFAULT PRIMARY CONTROL ROOM

Fig 5.06. The original configuration of the TARDIS control room featuring the original 'analogue-themed' instrument panel, the fault locator and a wall-mounted scanner monitor.

FIG 5.07. ESSENTIAL CONTROLS ON THE DEFAULT CONSOLE UNIT.

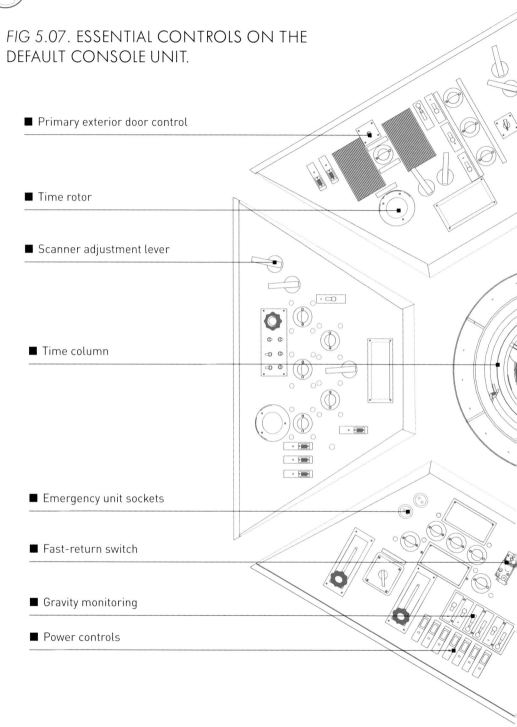

■ Primary exterior door control

■ Time rotor

■ Scanner adjustment lever

■ Time column

■ Emergency unit sockets

■ Fast-return switch

■ Gravity monitoring

■ Power controls

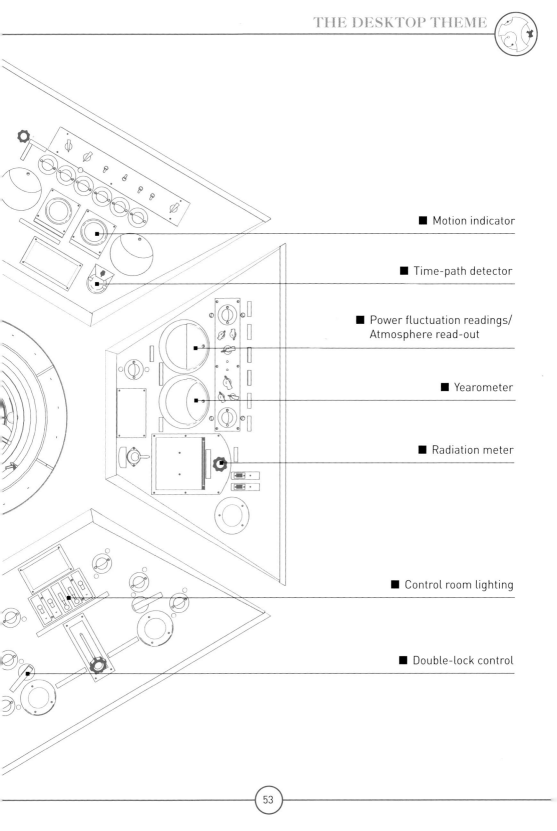

■ Motion indicator

■ Time-path detector

■ Power fluctuation readings/
Atmosphere read-out

■ Yearometer

■ Radiation meter

■ Control room lighting

■ Double-lock control

INITIAL UPDATE

Fig 5.08. A new version of the
primary control room with
updated control deck and new
roundels.

THE SECONDARY CONTROL ROOM

Fig 5.09. Alternative control chamber that can be relinked to the external doors. Used when the primary control room is closed for maintenance.

THE CONSOLE –
CONTROLS & FUNCTIONS

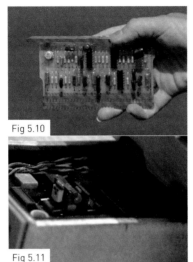

Fig 5.10

fig 5.10. The comparator.

fig 5.11. The temporal stabiliser.

fig 5.12. Fluid Link 'K7'.

Fig 5.11

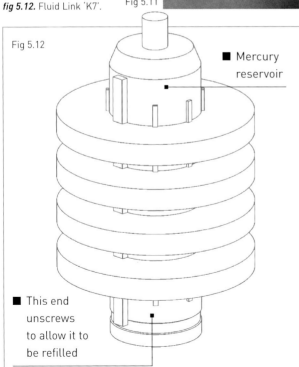

Fig 5.12

■ Mercury reservoir

■ This end unscrews to allow it to be refilled

MATERIALISATION

Before any TARDIS can be used the **briode nebuliser** has to be primed. This component stores a symbiotic link with Time Lord physiology – which means that once a Time Lord has activated the controls once, anyone can operate them.

There are a number of components that need to be kept in full working order to achieve dematerialisation. These include the **comparator**, the **temporal stabiliser** and, of course, the **dematerialisation circuit** itself (fig 5.10 and 5.11). It is important to make sure the **fluid links** (fig 5.12) are topped up with mercury. With careful modifications, however, it is possible to bypass the fluid links entirely.

On any capsule it will be found impossible to effect a smooth materialisation without first activating the **multiloop stabiliser**. Before you trigger materialisation it is also essential to engage the **synchronic feedback checking circuit**. In order to generate the appearance of the outer shell, the **visual stabiliser circuit** must be fully operational (see page 130: Section X – Troubleshooting).

When executing complex materialisation sequences involving hyperspatial force shields, you will find it useful to have a co-pilot who can check readings on the **gravity dilation meter** and the **warp oscilloscope**.

In addition to materialising on planets, the TARDIS can be set to **hover mode** – and hold a position, suspended in space. If evasive manoeuvres are required when in this pattern, the operator can reset the **coil cut out** and perform a **materialisation flip-flop**, which moves the TARDIS in and out of normal space to avoid imminent danger, such as debris or incoming missiles. This is only a temporary measure and a permanent, safe materialisation site should be found as soon as possible. Later models of the Type 40 are installed with an **automatic drift control** feature that allows the craft to suspend itself in space with absolute safety.

Rather than set a specific destination, it is possible to program the TARDIS to follow a trajectory through space-time. If you need the TARDIS to stop at any point along this path you can use either the **pause control** or the **drift compensators**. Care should be taken

■ This device is stored in a small dome on the TARDIS console

■ The recall disc

Fig 5.13

when using the pause control as it is deactivated by the TARDIS key when you re-enter the craft. If you remain outside and leave the key in the lock, the TARDIS may leave without you.

In such instances, it is useful to have a **Stattenheim remote control** (fig 5.13) to summon the TARDIS. Operating a TARDIS by remote control is a complex issue, however, and this feature is not a part of the default system.

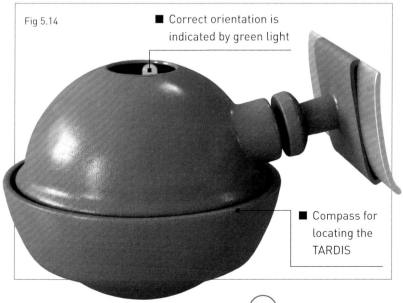

Fig 5.14

■ Correct orientation is indicated by green light

■ Compass for locating the TARDIS

fig 5.13. A Stattenheim remote control.

fig 5.14. A TARDIS Magnet can be keyed to a specific capsule so the operator can relocate it.

NAVIGATION

Of the many disciplines involved in operating a TARDIS, navigation is probably the most taxing. Plotting a course through the almost limitless expanse of time and space requires a great deal of precision – and there are many devices and processes that need to be mastered in order to turn up where and when you want to be. The navigational systems rely on systems such as the **helmic regulator**, the **linear calculator**, the **astro-sextant rectifier**, the **conceptual geometer**, the **orthogonal vector** and the **zig-zag plotter**. If you want to arrive in the correct century you must also ensure that the **lateral balance cones** are correctly aligned.

Operating in **basic mode** should make it easier to learn how to control the essential systems, but can leave the TARDIS vulnerable to external forces.

Key to maintaining a steady course is the **directional unit**. You must make sure that this unit is compatible with your model – if you substitute a directional unit intended for a more advanced model it is likely to burn out.

You can ensure that you turn up exactly where you plan by wiring the co-ordinates directly into the **space-time co-ordinate programmer** and confine the scope of travel by using a **temporal limiter**. You can also attempt to calculate a return journey to a previous destination using the **fast-return switch**.

During transit, progress through the vortex can be regulated using the **time rotor** and is reflected in the motion of the **time column** – the cylindrical structure in the centre of the console. If you are attempting to follow another vessel, you can lock onto their flight path using the **blue stabilisers**. Conversely, if you want to trace any vessel pursuing the TARDIS along the same space-time vector, use the **time path indicator**. In order to evade anyone tracking the TARDIS, a **randomiser** can be plugged into the system to generate unpredictable co-ordinates.

When your journey is complete, the flight computer should give a precise reading indicating where you have landed with the time period displayed on the **yearometer** (*fig 5.15*). It is possible to access local cartographical data through the **terrestrial navigation system** – this can be used as an additional means to verify where you have landed. It can also be employed, for a short period, to pilot the TARDIS in normal space, within a planet's atmosphere.

All TARDISes can be returned to Gallifrey using the **recall circuit**; any attempt to disable this function will further impede navigational precision.

Fig 5.15. The yearometer.

Fig 5.16. Cross section of the default console.

Fig 5.15

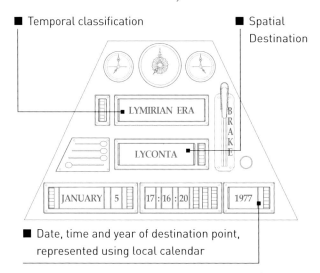

■ Temporal classification

■ Spatial Destination

LYMIRIAN ERA

B R A K E

LYCONTA

JANUARY 5   17 : 16 : 20   1977

■ Date, time and year of destination point, represented using local calendar

Fig 5.16

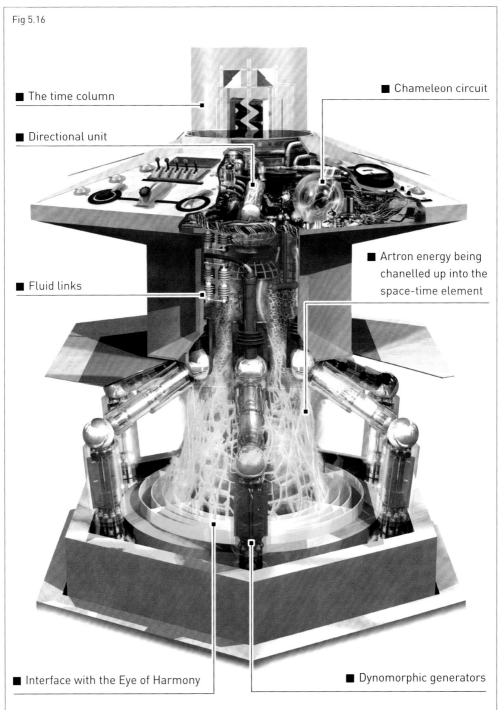

■ The time column

■ Chameleon circuit

■ Directional unit

■ Fluid links

■ Artron energy being chanelled up into the space-time element

■ Interface with the Eye of Harmony

■ Dynomorphic generators

MAJOR OVERHAUL

Fig 5.17. Reworking of the primary control room.
New central console with 'digital' interface.

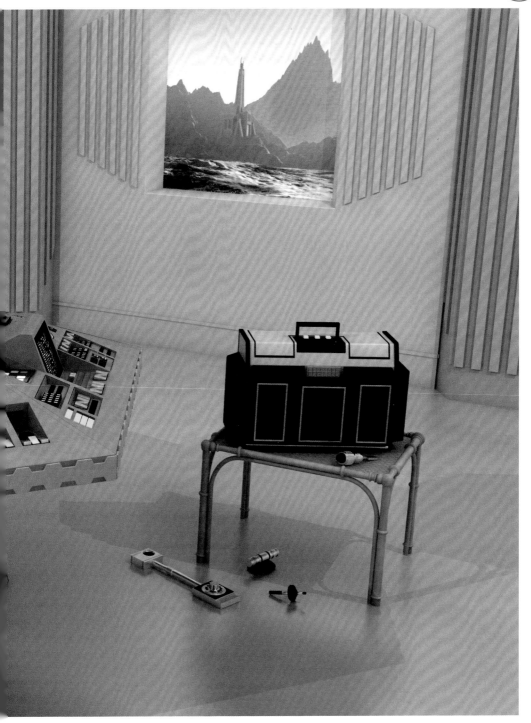

UNUSED DESKTOP THEME

Fig 5.18. One of the control rooms archived by the TARDIS's central systems that was never put into service.

Fig 5.19. Floorplan of the TARDIS prior to the Time War.

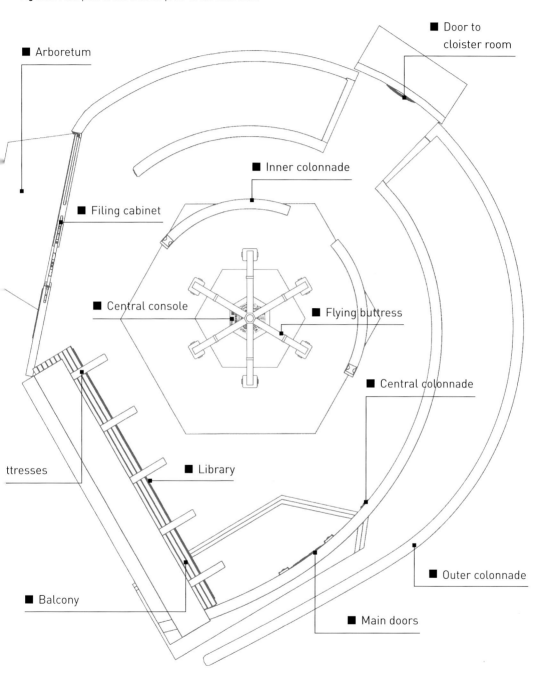

■ Door to
   cloister room

■ Arboretum

■ Inner colonnade

■ Filing cabinet

■ Central console

■ Flying buttress

■ Central colonnade

ttresses

■ Library

■ Outer colonnade

■ Balcony

■ Main doors

NEW DIRECTION

Fig 5.20. Comprehensive reworking of the control space, which adopted a consistent 'retro' design.

Fig 5.21

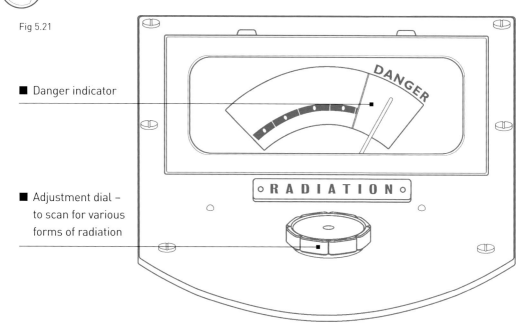

■ Danger indicator

■ Adjustment dial –
to scan for various
forms of radiation

SENSORS

The most useful sensor aboard the TARDIS is the external scanner (fig 5.22). This device uses an **interstitial beam synthesiser** to process what is outside, and that information is relayed to a monitor – mounted on the control room wall or console – using an **image translator**. The scanner only processes absolute values of the co-ordinates, which means the monitor may display inaccurate results if the TARDIS falls into an alternative universe.

If necessary it can be refocused to show rooms inside the ship.

This device can also be used as a **time scanner** to give a brief glimpse of the future – this might give you advance warning of any dangerous lifeforms you are about to encounter. It works on a similar principle to the **time-space visualiser**, which can provide a visual representation of anywhere in time and space.

In additional to visual sensors, there are a series of instruments that analyse the external atmosphere, including a **radiation detector** (fig 5.21).

The **signal conversion unit** can lock onto the frequency of psychic energy. The **deep scan** function can detect cracks in the fabric of time and space. The TARDIS also contains a **bio-scanner** (fig 5.23) that is used to provide a medical analysis of those on board.

Fig 5.22   Fig 5.23

POWER

All of the TARDIS systems are powered by the Eye of Harmony (fig 5.24), which fuels the engines and drives all other native Time Lord technology. This energy is stored and channelled in a number of different ways, using various components and processes.

The **dynomorphic generator** is a vital system that harnesses the colossal forces within the Eye and uses them to generate power. Transitional elements such as **Zeiton 7** are then used to maintain the alignment of the **transpower system** and create orbital energy. If reserves of transitional elements fall below a critical level, then the TARDIS engines may stall. In these situations the **emergency power booster** can be used to bypass any failing systems, providing enough power to reach safety (and to stock up on supplies of Zeiton 7).

If there is a power drain for some other reason you should be able to use the **emergency storage cells**.

Power throttling to the **parametric engines** is provided by the **velocity regulator** and the **quantum** and **atom accelerators**. The **orthogonal engine filters** ensure that the engines run at optimum efficiency. Engine temperature is regulated by the **thermal couplings** and the **thermal buffers**.

Care should be taken when routing power. Incorrect channelling of power can result in symbolic resonance in the **tachoid time crystal** — which will result in the TARDIS being unable to land. If the **reverse bias** is activated in full flight, a chain reaction will be triggered that will result in a huge explosion.

Any power exchange between the TARDIS and the space-time vortex is regulated by the **main space-time element**. This major component, fixed in the base of the console, is often removed if technicians wish to render the TARDIS inoperable.

Fig 5.24

Fig 5.21. The radiation detector.

Fig 5.22. The TARDIS scanner.

Fig 5.23. Bio-scanner.

Fig 5.24. The Eye of Harmony.

DIMENSIONAL CONTROLS

By default, the TARDIS maintains an interior space many, many times larger than its outer shell. The **dimensional control unit**, however, can be used to proportionally scale the interior space, such that it appears enlarged or shrunk relative to its usual size. Removing the **time vector generator** will result in an apparently empty shell – with the dimensions inside your craft matching those on the outside.

The **relative dimensional stabiliser** is used to cross the dimensional barrier between internal and external dimensions. It can also be employed to make any object – or lifeform – as large or as small as you wish.

The **friction contrafibulators**, meanwhile, are used to stabilise the control room space when switching between desktop themes.

COMMUNICATION DEVICES

The TARDIS is fitted with a **voice visual interface**. When it chooses, the interface can be used by the TARDIS central systems to communicate information to those aboard using a hologram projection of someone they trust (fig 5.25). This system can also be utilised by the operator to record messages – it can, for instance, be used to alert passengers to the activation of various security protocols or emergency programs.

Fig 5.25

Fig 5.25. The voice visual interface as it appeared to the Doctor's companion Rose Tyler.

Fig 5.26a. Sending a message to the Time Lords.

Fig 5.26b. Communicating with the navigational systems using the telepathic circuits.

Fig 5.26a

Fig 5.26b

Messages can be broadcast over long distances outside of the TARDIS by using the **light speed override**. Messages can also be sent and received using the **telepathic circuits** (*fig 5.26a* and *5.26b*). A **telepathic field** generated by the circuits can also be used to translate languages, enabling ease of communication on alien planets (for full details see Section VIII – The Telepathic Circuits).

Most important of all, however, is the **mark three emergency transceiver** (*fig 5.27*). This device, primarily used to send and receive distress signals, should be kept to hand at all times to receive vital communications from Gallifrey.

DATA BANKS

The **memory core** of the TARDIS contains knowledge that will be vital when travelling beyond Gallifrey. Specific dangers that you might encounter are listed in the **Record of Rassilon** – stored on the earliest section of the data core. More generic information can be accessed through the **TARDIS information system**.

As seen in the periodic updates to this user's guide, the TARDIS also keeps a log of all its previous journeys.

Fig 5.27

Fig 5.27. The mark three emergency transceiver.

Fig 5.28. Cross section of the console prior to the Time War.

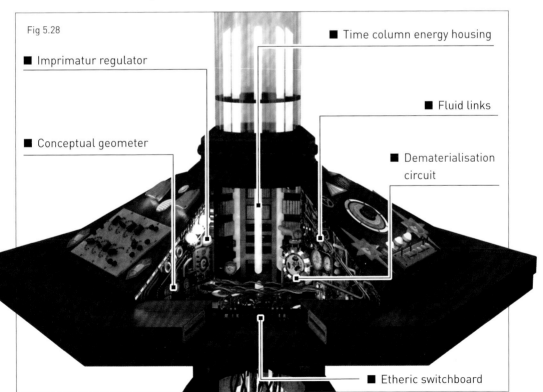

Fig 5.28

■ Imprimatur regulator

■ Conceptual geometer

■ Time column energy housing

■ Fluid links

■ Dematerialisation circuit

■ Etheric switchboard

TIME WAR CONTROL DECK

Fig 5.29. The TARDIS control room as it was fitted for battle during the Great Time War.

POST-TIME-WAR UPDATE

Fig 5.30. The refit of the control room in the immediate aftermath of the Time War.

TARDIS FOR A NEW DOCTOR

Fig 5.31. Replacement control room fashioned to succeed the previous chamber that was destroyed during the Doctor's regeneration.

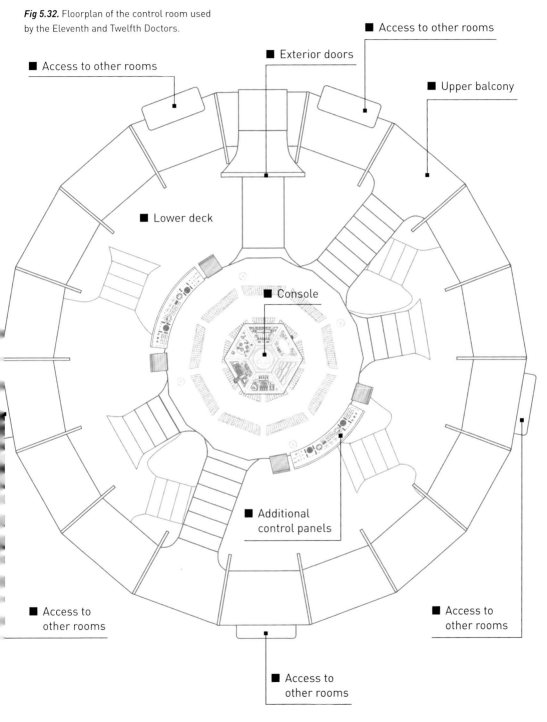

Fig 5.32. Floorplan of the control room used by the Eleventh and Twelfth Doctors.

■ Access to other rooms

■ Access to other rooms

■ Exterior doors

■ Upper balcony

■ Lower deck

■ Console

■ Additional control panels

■ Access to other rooms

■ Access to other rooms

■ Access to other rooms

MODERNIST REVIVAL

Fig 5.33. A new, multi-level control room, with a return to a more traditional control console.

REVISED VERSION

Fig 5.34. Changes to this version of the control area made by the Twelfth Doctor.

FIG 5.35. ESSENTIAL CONTROLS ON ONE OF THE RECONFIGURED CONSOLE UNITS.

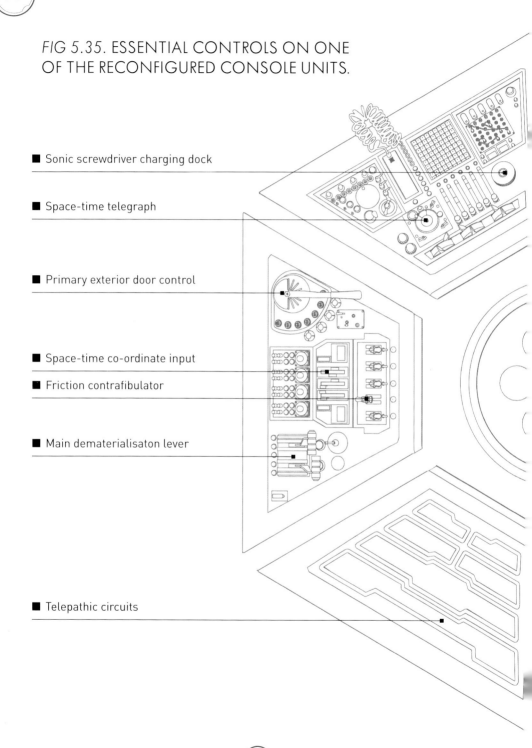

■ Sonic screwdriver charging dock

■ Space-time telegraph

■ Primary exterior door control

■ Space-time co-ordinate input

■ Friction contrafibulator

■ Main dematerialisaton lever

■ Telepathic circuits

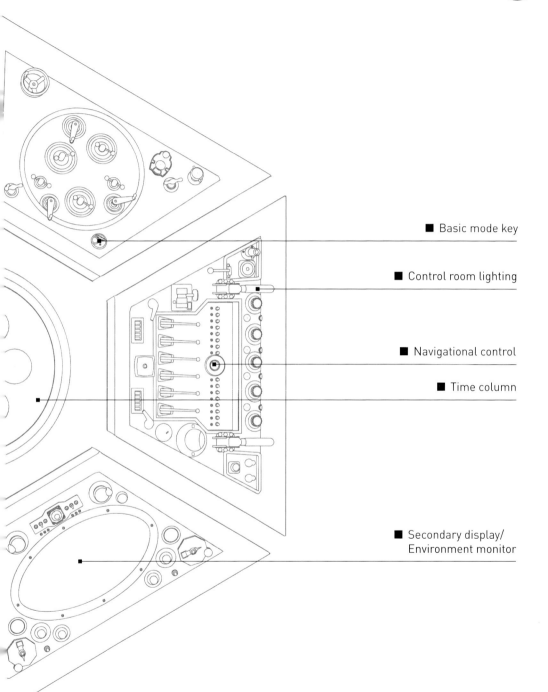

■ Basic mode key

■ Control room lighting

■ Navigational control

■ Time column

■ Secondary display/
Environment monitor

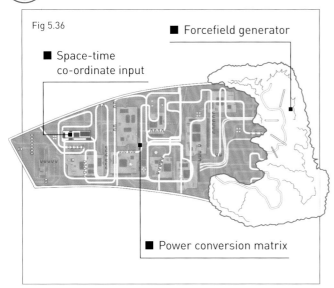

Fig 5.36

■ Forcefield generator

■ Space-time co-ordinate input

■ Power conversion matrix

FIELD GENERATORS

The **primary defence shield** is generated by the **force field generator** and can form an impregnable barrier around the ship. (For a full explanation see page 102: Section VII – Force Fields.)

It is possible to increase the functionality of the force field by connecting the system up to a **tribo-physical waveform macro-kinetic extrapolator** (fig 5.36) – a kind of pan-dimensional surfboard that can withstand extraordinary forces.

Obviously, it is preferable not to have to rely on a force field holding. Detection can be avoided by putting the outer

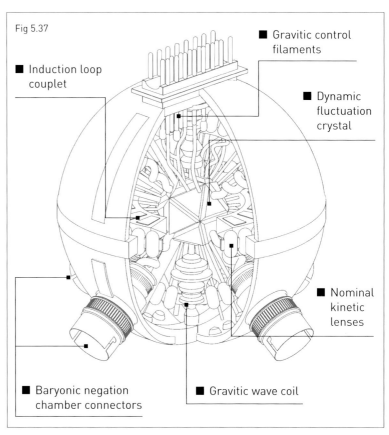

Fig 5.37

■ Induction loop couplet

■ Gravitic control filaments

■ Dynamic fluctuation crystal

■ Nominal kinetic lenses

■ Baryonic negation chamber connectors

■ Gravitic wave coil

Fig 5.36. The tribo-physical waveform macro-kinetic extrapolator.

Fig 5.37. The gravitic anomaliser.

Fig 5.38a. The TARDIS is attacked triggering the Hostile Action Displacement system.

Fig 5.38b. The TARDIS is reassembled after the Hostile Action Dispersal system was used.

Fig 5.39. Claims that the TARDIS interior exists in a 'state of temporal grace' turn out to be a clever lie.

shield on invisible – although this puts a huge drain on the power systems. If the TARDIS is in immediate danger, it can always move itself if the operator has remembered to set the **HADS** (fig 5.38). This is the Hostile Action Displacement/ Dispersal System, and can be used to move the TARDIS a short distance away or hold it in limbo until it is recalled. Be warned that if the drift compensators are open, the HADS may move the TARDIS further away than anticipated.

In order for telepathic communications to be received the force barrier needs to be lowered – a mental projection of sufficient force to penetrate the shields is simply beyond imagination, and would need to bypass the **relative continuum stabiliser**.

Inside the TARDIS, the **relative dimensional stabiliser field** will make it impossible to operate Gallifreyan patrol stasers. Time Lord engineers have attempted to extend this principle and create an environment of **temporal grace** within the TARDIS – where guns can't be fired and occupants can't be harmed. In practice, the implementation of this system has proved problematic (fig 5.39).

The force generators also have a number of other practical uses. The **gravitic anomaliser** (fig 5.37) generates a localised artificial gravity field – useful if you're trying to escape the gravity well of a black hole.

The **vortex drive** can create an anti-gravity spiral to guide the path of other vessels. This process, when carefully calibrated by auxiliary processing systems, can even be used to move

DATA RETRIEVAL

Fig 5.38a

Fig 5.38b

planets. Given the requisite amount of time to process the relevant data, the TARDIS system can also place a whole planet in stasis, removing it from normal space and freezing it at a single point in time.

Fig 5.39

AUXILIARY FUNCTIONS

The TARDIS systems are very efficient and recycle any waste products. Anything that can't be processed, however, is sent to the waste tank on deck seven. There is a button on the console that can be used to evacuate the tank.

The vessel's infinite power reserves can also be used to sustain – or even fabricate – other systems. By linking the **molecular stabiliser** up to the circuit frequency modulator of a computer system you can effect an entire circuit regeneration – useful for repairing broken smart phones and robot dogs. The **architectural reconfiguration system** meanwhile will reconstruct particles to your needs and can, in principle, build any machine you might require.

Under certain conditions, the TARDIS can compensate for temporal paradoxes using the **reality compensators** and the **doomsday bumpers**. You can even use the TARDIS systems to cook by exposing food to the time winds (fig 5.40).

Fig 5.40. Using the TARDIS as an oven.

Fig 5.41. A fatal crash of the TARDIS systems.

Fig 5.42. Countdown to self-destruct.

Fig 5.43. Cross section of console used by the Twelfth Doctor.

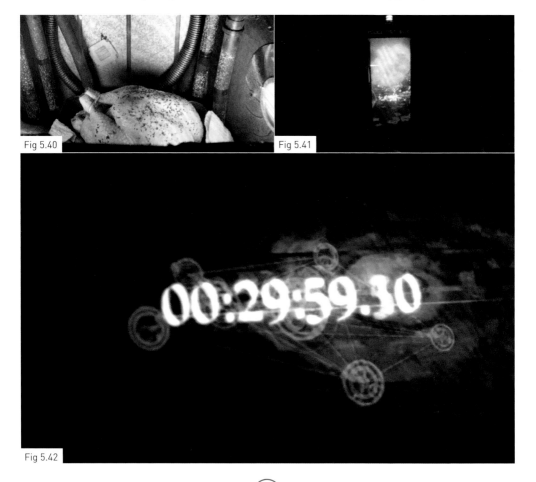

Fig 5.40

Fig 5.41

Fig 5.42

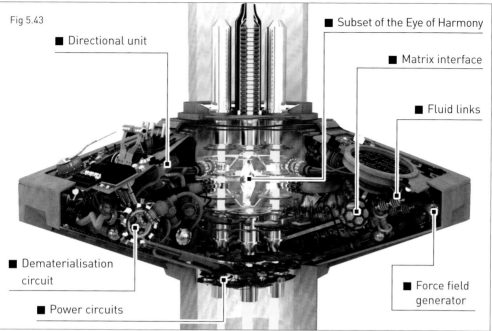

Fig 5.43

■ Directional unit

■ Subset of the Eye of Harmony

■ Matrix interface

■ Fluid links

■ Dematerialisation circuit

■ Power circuits

■ Force field generator

EMERGENCY SYSTEMS

Travellers will be alerted to calamitous situations by the **cloister bell** ringing. The TARDIS is fitted with a full array of emergency systems to employ in these circumstances — ranging from the careful monitoring of volatile circuits by the **fault locator** to entering **siege mode** where the entire vessel goes into lockdown (see page 136: Section X — Troubleshooting: Case Studies).

In cases when the TARDIS is under immediate threat it can be powered down manually by folding back the **omega configuration**, halting the **exponential cross-field**, closing the **pathways to conditional states seven to seventeen**, and ending the **main** and **auxiliary drive**.

One instance that can cause a fatal crash of the TARDIS systems is a **multiple operations failure** (fig 5.41). In certain cases, if the TARDIS is in danger of breaking up, the **failsafe** system will kick in, and it will latch onto the nearest passing spaceship.

If there is any chance that the TARDIS might fall into the hands of a dangerous third party, then the pilot should consider activating the **self-destruct** (fig 5.42).

Another drastic option when the TARDIS is under threat is to take it out of time and space — out of reality altogether, into a conceptual realm — using the **emergency unit**.

If all else fails, there is a switch on the console helpfully labelled **extreme emergency** — which can, among other things, rescue people stranded in the space-time vortex. Following particularly catastrophic events, the TARDIS can rewrite the history of an entire day, by sending a **big friendly button** through a rift in time to create a temporal diversion.

CURRENT DESKTOP THEME

Fig 5.44. Replacement control room fashioned to succeed the previous chamber that was destroyed during the Doctor's regeneration.

THE LATEST TARDIS INTERIOR

The TARDIS is more than a machine. It needs coaxing, persuading, encouraging… Any new interface generated will take time to reveal its secrets. Users will only uncover its full potential over the course of time.

The current desktop theme, in common with many recent configurations, is a dark, atmospheric chamber – on this occasion lit in blue and orange. The walls are constructed from a series of interlocking and overlapping steel panels with large circles cut from them. Giant, glowing crystalline pillars surround the central control console.

The floor is decorated with an elaborate hexagonal design, leading up to the exterior doors. For the first time, the reverse of three sides of the police box exterior are part of the interior dimensions, so it might appear as if the inside of the TARDIS is accessed through the back wall – rather than it being inside the box.

The time column in the new console is replaced by another crystalline structure, the console itself being a skeletal construction – a framework of tubes, pipes and supporting brackets that is lit from within. This circular control panel is divided into six panels, featuring a variety of instruments including an hourglass timer.

This latest manifestation of the primary control space features a number of elements that are reminiscent of the previous control rooms – and is faithful to the basic template used throughout the TARDIS' long service.

Overall, however, it is a distinctive remodelling. Once all primary systems have been run in, the operator will discover increased functionality and a new dynamic between them and their craft.

It's unlikely to be the last time this Type 40 TARDIS is refitted with a dramatic new interior.

Fig 5.45: The entrance to the current control space.
Fig 5.46: New roundels.

Fig 5.45

Fig 5.46

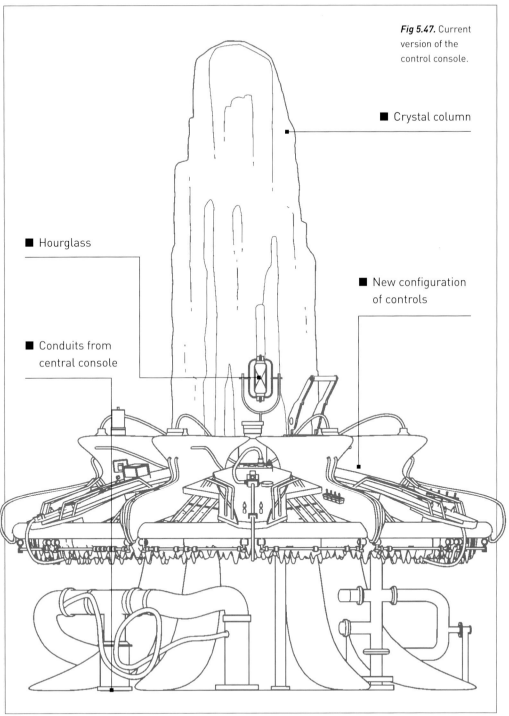

Fig 5.47. Current version of the control console.

■ Crystal column

■ Hourglass

■ New configuration of controls

■ Conduits from central console

CASE STUDY

THE TIME WAR INCIDENT

TELEPATHIC CIRCUIT MEMORY NODE RETRIEVAL
NODE: 50
SPATIAL CO-ORDINATES: Earth (Terra) / Gallifrey.
TEMPORAL CO-ORDINATES: Local Dateline: 20th Century / Time Lock
TARDIS CREW: The War Doctor (Gallifreyan), The Tenth Doctor (Gallifreyan),
The Eleventh Doctor (Gallifreyan), Clara Oswald (Terran).

NOTES:
Whilst the basic construction of all TARDISes begins with their 'birth' and 'growth' at the Black Hole shipyards and defaults to organic patterns (see page 12: Section I — Construction), the layout and appearance of the interior of all Type 40 capsules can be altered using the Architectural Configuration System to suit the different styles and moods of individual operators.

Most Time Lords are happy to leave their TARDIS settings in factory basic mode, however some of the more flamboyant characters from Gallifreyan history have chosen to synchronise

their pedestrian infrastructures in line with their own personality traits. This 'desktop theme' (see Index File: Twentieth Century Terran Computer slang) is telepathically linked to the operator's psyche, and will automatically set the internal parameters accordingly. Time Lords with dangerous personality traits such as the self-styled 'Master' and 'Rani' appear to adversely affect the circuits of their Capsules and their TARDISes reconfigure themselves in patterns and colour schemes seemingly outside the usual factory parameters (see page 150, Appendix – Other TARDISes are Available).

Please note that two or more Time Lords with high levels of Artron energy, or more than one incarnation from an individual timestream, occupying the same control room may cause the Architectural Configuration System to alternate between settings as it tries to compensate for all requested patterns. To avoid the confusion that this causes to the TARDIS telepathic matrix, Time Lords are requested to allocate one individual as the 'designated architectural theme driver'.

The most common variant on the basic 'white' theme is the 'coral' desktop theme, leaving

CASE STUDY

TARDIS architecture in its 'raw' organic state. In the years directly following the Time War, the Doctor was forced to make repairs to this TARDIS without the benefit of access to Gallifreyan technology and, as a result, the console in particular became something of a hybrid, with different technology from a variety of civilisations sitting alongside the original controls.

Systems damage when the Tenth Doctor regenerated resulted in TARDIS architectural systems replicating some of these non-Gallifreyan components into the new console room configuration. Later, however, the Doctor deleted this theme and settled on an architectural layout for both console room and corridors that resembled the initial factory settings far more closely.

(Files regarding the exact circumstances of this event are restricted to members of the High Council and War Council, but the unofficial memoir 'Thirteen of Them: I Didn't Know When I Was Well Off' by General Kenossium gives enough basic information.)

Whilst this flouting of the First Law of Time was unauthorised, the Doctor's actions by collaborating with his previous incarnations resulted in him being able to freeze Gallifrey in a single moment of time, dimensionally shifted from the universe and held in stasis. Although the calculations involved in freezing a planet in this way are in theory too complex to be undertaken within one lifetime, the Doctor managed it by using the TARDIS's telepathic circuits (See page 98: The Telepathic Circuits) to circumvent the Blinovich Limitation Effect and run the calculations across all thirteen incarnations of himself so that his tenth and eleventh incarnations had access to that information at the right moment.

During the incident in which it seems that the Doctor collaborated with earlier versions of himself in order to change the events surrounding the siege of Gallifrey at the end of the Great Time War, three distinct versions of the Doctor entered the control room at the same time, causing this capsule to alternate between the different variants of internal configuration that each of the Doctors had set as 'their' pattern.

CORRIDORS OF ETERNITY

It would be impossible to enumerate the thousands of chambers and connecting passageways within the TARDIS. These rooms can also be altered at will using the architectural configuration systems. (These systems can be used to restructure any interior space. Converting energy to matter, the TARDIS generates any matter that is native to the ship. Conversely, if additional power is needed, rooms can be deleted to generate energy.)

Below is a list of some of the most notable rooms.

WORKING AREAS

The Eye of Harmony: A chamber, located at the centre of the TARDIS's interior space, that houses a trans-dimensional link to the Eye of Harmony – the source of all the ship's power (fig 6.01).

The architectural configuration chamber: This area is composed of the TARDIS's basic genetic material. The systems contained here are, in the crude monetary value maintained in other cultures, priceless – as they can spontaneously generate any physical form.

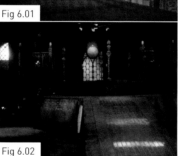

Fig 6.01

Fig 6.02

Fig 6.01. The entry point to the Eye of Harmony.

Fig 6.02. The cloister room: an additional access point.

Fig 6.03. The entrance to the engine room.

Fig 6.03

The cloisters: A series of stone walkways, surrounding a courtyard, that lead to the cloister room. In case of emergencies, a bell in the cloisters rings to alert those on board to danger.

Within the cloister room itself is a secondary access point to the Eye of Harmony (fig 6.02).

The engine room: The TARDIS is able to protect this area using an illusory portal (fig 6.03) that will deter anyone unfamiliar with the TARDIS from approaching its core systems.

The power room: A small room that contains finely tuned mechanisms (fig 6.04) that measure power differentials inside and outside the TARDIS.

Ancillary power station: The ancillary power station contains the back-up generators. Like the engine room this area has the ability to camouflage itself (fig. 6.13).

Tool room: All the tools necessary to perform manual repairs to the TARDIS are stored here – such as the radiation wave meter.

Laboratory: The TARDIS has a fully equipped lab that can be used to analyse alien samples.

Workshops and Storeroom: The central workshop was used at one stage to build a demat gun – the ultimate weapon – that was instrumental in saving Gallifrey from invasion.

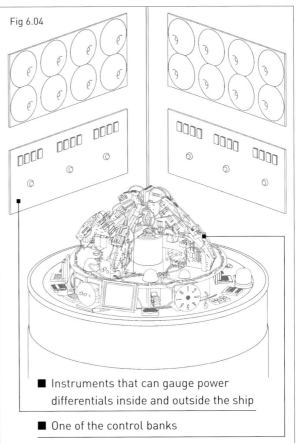

Fig 6.04

■ Instruments that can gauge power differentials inside and outside the ship

■ One of the control banks

Fig 6.05

Garage: Hangar where any additional vehicles for travels outside the TARDIS can be parked. The Doctor stores an anti-gravity motorcycle (fig 6.05) (that was ridden in the 2074 Anti-Grav Olympics) here.

Fig 6.04. Inside the power room.

Fig 6.05. The Doctor's anti-gravity motorcycle.

Fig 6.06

Fig 6.07

Fig 6.08

REST & RECREATION

Bedrooms: In the default configuration, the TARDIS has an area close to the primary control room containing a series of bunks useful for resting, and for sleep on short missions. An early update of the control area also contained a fold-down bed for similar purposes (fig 6.06). There is a selection of bedrooms that can be used by anyone staying on board for a longer period (eg fig 6.07). When the TARDIS was invaded by the malevolent entity known as House (see page 112: Section VIII – The Telepathic Circuits: Case Studies), all the bedrooms were deleted, and new ones had to be created.

Bathroom facilities: The TARDIS has a luxurious bathroom. It features a hologram of a leopard, encountered once by the Doctor's companion Clara Oswald. There are also toilet facilities, just past the macaroon dispenser, a short distance from the primary control room.

Wardrobe: The TARDIS's walk-in wardrobe has moved several times over the centuries to accommodate the ever-expanding number of outfits that were either fabricated by the TARDIS or acquired from places it has visited.

Initially, the wardrobe was stored in a series of small rooms. The Doctor often headed there after a regeneration to assemble a new look.

The refitted wardrobe (fig 6.08), used by the Tenth Doctor following his regeneration, was some distance from the control room – first left, second right, third on the left, straight ahead under the stairs, past the bins, the fifth door on the left. When the whole TARDIS was reconfigured, the wardrobe was moved closer to the control room – near to the helter skelter.

Rather than selecting garments here, the TARDIS can also project clothing directly onto the visual cortex of others, giving the appearance of wearing clothes when naked.

Fig 6.06. Temporary sleeping quarters.

Fig 6.07. Bedroom used by the Doctor's companions Nyssa and Tegan.

Fig 6.08. The refitted wardrobe where the Tenth Doctor found his clothes.

Fig 6.09

Kitchen: The kitchen is located quite a distance from the control chamber. In lieu of using the kitchen, TARDIS travellers can rely on the food machine (fig 6.10). This can serve up any food in the form of small white nutritional slices. And also water and milk.

The Doctor's companion Clara took an interest in the kitchen – having a fondness for making soufflés despite not being able to follow the simple instructions to cook a roast turkey.

Library: The TARDIS library (fig 6.09) is arranged over six storeys and contains books from many civilisations. The library contains a singularly Time Lord invention – bottled books: glass jars containing a purplish fluid that stores the text, when opened words evaporate in the air leaving an audible trace. The *Encyclopedia Gallifreya* is stored in this form.

Books from the library have been relocated all over the ship. The Seventh and Twelfth Doctors established a collection of particularly useful titles within the control room.

Swimming pool: The original TARDIS pool was jettisoned when it was found

to be leaking. Since then, however there have been a series of additional swimming pools installed.

The first of these ended up in the library when the TARDIS crash-landed following the Tenth Doctor's regeneration. The pool was re-instated and used as a safe landing point for the Doctor's associate River Song, when the TARDIS caught her falling from a skyscraper. The TARDIS materialised on its side, and she fell through the doors into the pool.

The Doctor deleted the swimming pool a second time – using it to generate extra energy in an attempt to leave the universe and enter another.

Since then, however, yet another pool has been installed.

Fig 6.09. The TARDIS library.

Fig 6.10. The food machine.

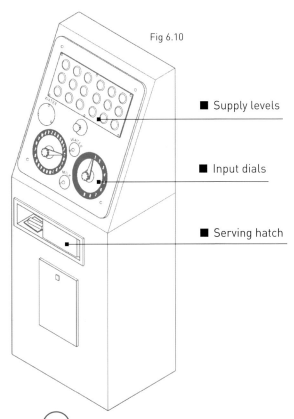

Fig 6.10

■ Supply levels

■ Input dials

■ Serving hatch

Fig 6.11

Fig 6.12

Fig 6.13

Squash court: The TARDIS has a series of squash courts. The Doctor deleted squash court seven to generate extra energy to leave the universe and head into another realm.

Karaoke bar: The Doctor considered sacrificing this room to generate the requisite energy to maintain a temporal paradox, when faced with the decision of choosing between a younger and older version of his companion Amy Pond.

Boot cupboard: Room close to the secondary control room where the Doctor keeps his boots (*fig 6.11*).

Cricket pavilion: Changing room (*fig 6.12*) where the Fifth Doctor found a new outfit.

Fig 6.11. The boot cupboard.

Fig 6.12. The cricket pavilion.

Fig 6.13. The art gallery, which acts as a front for the ancillary power station.

Art gallery: The Doctor disguised the ancillary power room as an art gallery including the Venus de Milo and works by artists Jan van Eyck, Turner and Matisse (*fig 6.13*).

Greenhouse: The TARDIS has a greenhouse that contains rare specimens from across the cosmos.

BODY & SOUL

Sickbay: The sickbay is located near the control room – up the stairs, left and left again.

It can be used to administer emergency medical attention, but it is advisable to seek help from a trained professional. If, for example, someone on board needs dental work, it is better that the TARDIS is taken somewhere where a qualified practitioner can be found.

Because expert assistance can be found by piloting the TARDIS to an applicable medical facility, the sickbay is not stocked with an inexhaustible supply of medicines. It may, for example, have a remedy that can cure a terminal blood clot in the brain, but might not have the necessary antibiotics to treat typhoid fever.

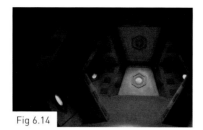

Fig 6.14

The Zero room: All rooms in the TARDIS show up on the architectural configurations indicators – except one. The Zero room is balanced to zero energy with respect to the world outside its four walls. These 'null interfaces' provide a neutral environment cut off from the rest of the universe – an ideal space for a Time Lord to recuperate after a problematic regeneration.

When a Time Lord's synapses are weak, they are like radio receivers, picking up all sorts of jumbled signals. The Zero room cuts out interference. The room even has its own gravity, which makes levitation possible.

The Doctor deleted the Zero room, to generate extra energy to escape from the gravitational forces produced by Event One (see page 98 – Case Study). With the Doctor still disorientated by his recent regeneration the remaining doors to the deleted room were used to construct a new Zero room – referred to as the Zero cabinet (fig 6.15).

Control centre – the Doctor's tomb: At the end of its operational lifespan the control room will be repurposed to contain an entry point to the complete timeline of its primary user – the Doctor. (See page 146: Section XI – Modifications: Case Study.)

VIRTUAL SPACES

Corridors: Although the endless corridors (eg fig 6.14) snaking through the interior space are a part of the solid fabric of the TARDIS, they can be diverted to create shortcuts or to redirect intruders. If the pedestrian infrastructure isn't stabilised, three people leaving a room by different exits can find themselves arriving at the same point.

Archived rooms: This TARDIS currently has about 30 desktop themes stored including some that haven't happened yet.

Echo rooms: The control room is the safest space aboard the TARDIS – and it can replicate itself any number of times to isolate passengers and keep them safe.

Fig 6.14. Another corridor design.

Fig 6.15. The Zero cabinet.

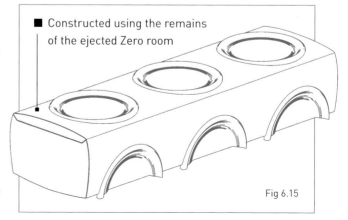

■ Constructed using the remains of the ejected Zero room

Fig 6.15

THE CASTROVALVA INCIDENT

TELEPATHIC CIRCUIT MEMORY NODE RETRIEVAL
NODE: 5Z/76
SPATIAL CO-ORDINATES: Centre of the Universe.
TEMPORAL CO-ORDINATES: Hydrogen Inrush – Event One.
TARDIS CREW: The Fifth Doctor (Gallifreyan), Tegan Jovanka (Terran),
Nyssa of Traken (Traken Union).

NOTES:
Whilst the Architectural Configuration System is primarily used to set the pedestrian infrastructure when a capsule is being fitted out in dry dock, it is possible to use the manual override to access this facility whilst in flight, although this procedure is not without its dangers and is not recommended other than in exceptional circumstances.

This node outlines a situation where the crew of this TARDIS, caught up in the Time Force of the space/time phenomena referred to as 'Event One' (an environment that would have exceeded the engineering tolerances of this model) had to delete sections of the primary infrastructure in order to generate enough thrust to break free.

With the Doctor temporarily incapacitated due to the regeneration trauma associated with

his fourth regeneration, the non-Gallifreyan occupants, Terran Tegan Jovanka and Nyssa of Traken, exposed themselves to significant danger by deleting approximately twenty-five percent of the internal volume. The fact that this procedure was carried out using manual override meant that the standard safeguard protocol ensuring that any living beings present in rooms about to be deleted are deposited in the primary control room was non-functional. Manual override also means that there are no safeguards against accidental deletion of the primary console room itself.

(Whilst there is no example on record of what might happen in the event of a primary control room being deleted, it is generally theorised that this would result in destruction of the TARDIS. If this occurred whilst within the confines of the space/time vortex, then there is a possibility that it could trigger a Total Event Collapse (see Section IX: Invalidating the Warranty. Node 5/31:13.)

Whilst the procedure was ultimately successful, and this capsule successfully broke through from Event One without sustaining any damage, use of this function did result in the deletion of the TARDIS Zero room, which was essential to the Doctor's wellbeing during this particular regeneration event.

Although Tegan and Nyssa managed to find a suitable uncomplicated environment in which the Doctor could complete his regeneration and recover, the location turned out to be a space/time trap constructed by the Master using the mathematical skills of the Doctor's Alzarian companion Adric to create a city using Block Transfer Computation (see Index File: Logopolis).

Ultimately the city of Castrovalva collapsed in on itself due to dimensional instabilities that had been deliberately included within its makeup. Whilst the time that he spent in Castrovalva initially appeared to aid the Doctor's regeneration, it is likely that his full recovery can actually be attributed to the fact that it had been possible to construct a 'Zero cabinet' from the doors of the deleted Zero room, and that this cabinet retained enough of the healing properties required to allow the regeneration to stabilise.

It must be stressed once again that the use of the Architectural Configuration System should not be attempted when the capsule is in flight mode.

SUB-NODE RETRIEVAL
NODE: 5V/41
SPATIAL CO-ORDINATES: Earth (Terra).
TEMPORAL CO-ORDINATES: Local
Dateline: 20th Century
TARDIS CREW: The Fourth Doctor
(Gallifreyan), Adric (Alzarian).

NOTES:
Just prior to the events outlined above, the fourth incarnation of the Doctor used this 'room jettison' facility to escape a localised gravity bubble caused by materialising one capsule inside another (see Case Study with this reference in Section X). Escape from this bubble proved impossible using available power, and so the Doctor released additional energy by using the Architectural Configuration System to delete rooms, converting mass to energy.

The Eleventh Doctor also used the method of acquiring additional power in order to remove this TARDIS from the Universe whilst following a distress signal, and yet again in order to return the TARDIS to our universe (see Section VIII: Telepathic Circuits Node 7/33.04).

FORCE FIELDS

When properly maintained, the TARDIS is indestructible. If the systems aren't kept in perfect working order or the force shields are shut down, however, it is vulnerable to external forces. Full details of extreme circumstances that will threaten the integrity of the craft can be found in Section IX – Invalidating the Warranty.

The force field can protect the TARDIS if it falls from a great height or if it is attacked by missiles, as well as generally insulate it against the vacuum of space or the time winds produced within the space-time vortex. The force field can also be extended for observing outer space through the main doors, and for providing protection for anyone attached to the outer shell as the TARDIS travels through the vortex (fig 7.01 and 7.02).

In exceptional circumstances, the shields of this ship can be extruded to create a corridor through the vacuum of space between the TARDIS and another ship.

TRACTOR BEAM

As well as being used to keep the TARDIS crew safe, the field generators can also

Fig 7.01

Fig 7.02

Fig 7.01. The Doctor's companion Clara Oswald caught in the TARDIS's dematerialisation field.

Fig 7.02. The Doctor's friend Captain Jack hitches a ride to the end of the universe.

be used as a tractor beam: providing a safe landing for another vessel that is out of control, dragging a vessel away from the gravity well of a black hole and even pulling a planet through space (see page 106: Case Studies).

Although these systems can also be used to balance external forces, there are devices that can drag the TARDIS itself off course. A navigational guidance system distorter, for example, could be used to force a TARDIS to land on the planet it is being operated from.

Beyond providing a force shield and working as a tractor beam, the force field generator (fig 7.03) can also create a barrier between the universes of matter and anti-matter.

TIME LOOPS

The TARDIS is equally capable of applying a temporal force as it is a physical one. That is to say its generators can bend time around an object. This can be used to force another vessel into a time loop – so that it repeatedly passes through the same points in time and space.

When facing destruction, the TARDIS, at its own discretion, is even capable of preserving personnel and vital systems by placing parts of itself in a time loop.

Fig 7.03. The Force Field Generator.

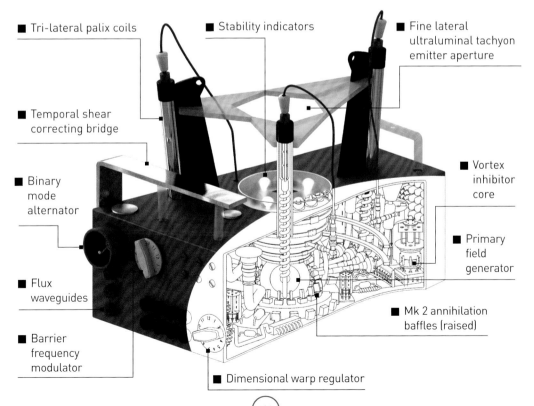

- Tri-lateral palix coils
- Stability indicators
- Fine lateral ultraluminal tachyon emitter aperture
- Temporal shear correcting bridge
- Binary mode alternator
- Vortex inhibitor core
- Flux waveguides
- Primary field generator
- Barrier frequency modulator
- Mk 2 annihilation baffles (raised)
- Dimensional warp regulator

THE CHLORIS INCIDENT

TELEPATHIC CIRCUIT MEMORY NODE RETRIEVAL
NODE: 5G / 11
SPATIAL CO-ORDINATES: Chloris
TEMPORAL CO-ORDINATES: Local Dateline: 13th Century
TARDIS CREW: The Fourth Doctor (Gallifreyan), Romanadvoratrelundar –
second incarnation (Gallifreyan), K-9 (Artificial Intelligence).

NOTES:
Mark Three Emergency Transceivers are fitted as standard equipment aboard all Type 40 Time Capsules. However, the transceiver on-board this TARDIS was disconnected by the Doctor as an attempt to avoid receiving emergency transmissions from Gallifrey. (NB: Disconnection of this device is prohibited, and disregard for this instruction carries a custodial sentence. On no account should TARDIS operators leave the localised spatial co-ordinates of Gallifrey without ensuring that this equipment is fully charged and operational.)

Upon reconnection of the transceiver to the console, the TARDIS received an intergalactic distress signal from a Tythonian ambassador trapped on the planet Chloris. After nearly fifteen years trying to secure the release of their ambassador, the Tythonian Government finally declared war on Chloris and, despite Shadow

Proclamation objections on the grounds of excessive retaliation, dispatched a neutron star to destroy Chloris's sun.

Having secured Erato's release, the Doctor persuaded him to neutralise the threat of the neutron star by utilising the Tythonians' natural ability to weave a thin shell of aluminium around it. In order to hold the star steady while the ambassador spun his web, the Doctor made use of the TARDIS tractor beam.

TARDIS tractor beams are capable of generating extremely powerful gravitational fields, however, when being used to stabilise objects with a radius in excess of 10 kilometres (6.2 miles) and a mass greater than 3 solar masses they must only be used in short bursts to avoid significant damage to time-field instrumentation.

Nonetheless, the Doctor's plan was successful and the neutron star was successfully diverted from the Chloris system.

CASE STUDY

THE PLANETARY RELOCATION INCIDENT

TELEPATHIC CIRCUIT MEMORY NODE RETRIEVAL
NODE: 4/30:12/13
SPATIAL CO-ORDINATES: Earth (Terra) / The Medusa Cascade.
TEMPORAL CO-ORDINATES: Local Dateline: 21st Century.
TARDIS CREW: The Tenth Doctor (Gallifreyan), meta-crisis Doctor-variant
(Gallifreyan / Terran hybrid), Donna Noble (Terran), Captain Jack Harkness (Terran),
Sarah Jane Smith (Terran), Mickey Smith (Terran), Jackie Tyler (Terran).

NOTES:

Whist it *is* possible to navigate a Type 40 Capsule
with a single experienced pilot, it must be noted
that efficient operation can only be achieved with
a full crew complement of six.

Outside of factory testing, the only time
that this capsule has been operated in anything
approaching the correct manner has been when it
was used to return the planet Earth to its original
position after the Daleks had relocated it in time
and space during their attempt to construct a
'reality bomb'.

Led by Davros and advised by Dalek Caan
(see Index File: The Cult of Skaro) the Daleks had
attempted to create a compression field capable
of cancelling the electrical energy of atoms. The
resulting waveform had the potential to destroy
all matter in every universe. In order to create
a planetary engine capable of transmitting that
wave form the Daleks had scooped 27 planets
from positions across the space-time continuum
and placed them in a self-stabilising configuration
inside the Medusa Cascade, an inter-universal
rift (see Shadow Proclamation Files: Planetary
Relocation Incident).

Whilst the Doctor and his associates were
successful in thwarting the Dalek plan and returning
most of the planets to their correct space/time

co-ordinates, there was insufficient power to return the planet Earth to its correct location and the Doctor was forced to use the TARDIS tractor beam to physically pull the planet back into place.

Because of the problems inherent with towing an object with that mass for such a long period, whilst also using TARDIS systems to maintain a coherent atmospheric shell, the Doctor made use of the Rift Manipulator at the Torchwood Base in Cardiff to send additional Rift energy to the TARDIS. He also made use of a sentient Xylock

crystal embedded in the super computer referred to as Mister Smith to harness the energy from the Cardiff Rift and loop it around the TARDIS by providing remote access to this capsule's base code numerals. (Please note: access to TARDIS base code numerals should be restricted to capsule operators and Gallifreyan technicians only. Sharing that access data with inferior AI, or with computer systems that do not have the necessary firewall protection, exposes TARDIS systems to attack by non-Gallifreyan viruses and can result in a breach of personal bio-data extract information. Please refer to

the latest version of the Academies Data Protection Policy.)

Having a full complement of crew operating each panel of the console simultaneously, coupled with the additional power from the Rift allowed the TARDIS to operate at maximum efficiency and the procedure was totally successful.

TARDIS operators should check with their designated flight control staff in advance of any journey in order to check that a sufficient number of trained crew are available, and if not whether operational requirements can be carried out by merging crews with that of another TT Capsule.

THE TELEPATHIC CIRCUITS

The telepathic circuits form a symbiotic link between a TARDIS and its operator. This is necessary to make use of the mulit-functional controls on the console. It is also helpful when navigating. To supplement any programmed co-ordinates, the telepathic circuits can gather extra data about the intended destination and calculate an optimum point to land.

Individuals with a special bond with the TARDIS may further benefit from this symbiotic link. The TARDIS can use the telepathic circuits to transfer the knowledge necessary to operate the TARDIS.

In contrast, any individual who exhibits signs of being a temporal anomaly – being either a fixed point in time, or existing in multiple timestreams –will be rejected by the TARDIS systems (fig 8.01 and 8.02).

The telepathic circuits can be used to send psychic messages within the space-time vortex (see p112: Case Studies). The system can also be accessed directly,

Fig 8.01

Fig 8.02

Fig 8.01. Captain Jack – a temporal anomaly after being brought back to life.

Fig 8.02. The TARDIS tolerated Clara Oswald's anomalous nature.

Fig 8.03. An early presentation of the telepathic controls.

Fig 8.03

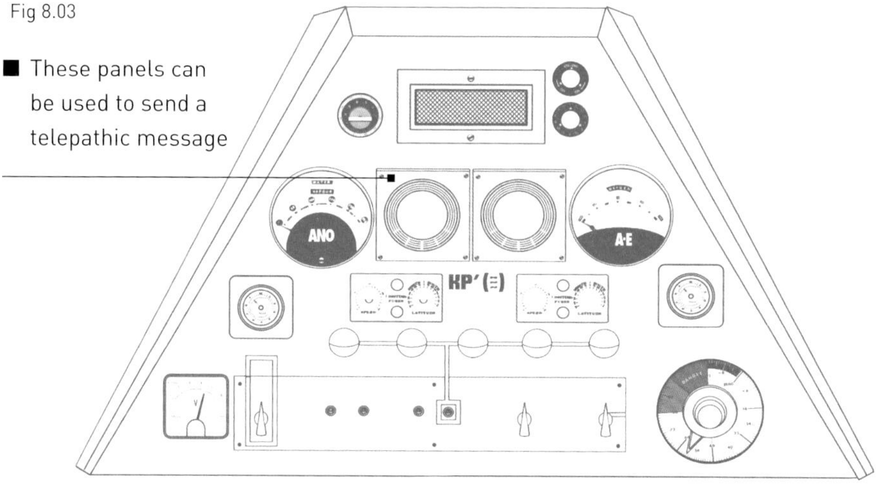

■ These panels can be used to send a telepathic message

through the TARDIS console (*fig 8.03* and *8.07*). Contact with the panels can allow an individual to broadcast a message through time and space, or to pilot the ship using only memories (see page 116: Case Studies).

TRANSLATION

One of the other beneficial processes provided by the telepathic circuits is translation. It's a Time Lord gift. The union of a Time Lord and the TARDIS's telepathic field allows anyone within range to communicate – hearing their own language when others speak. This function can be misused. It is possible to adjust the translation matrix to detect someone's speech, scramble it, send it back, and make it sound as if they are talking backwards.

The translation matrix also works on writing (*fig 8.04*) – with words appearing as if they are written in the observer's native language. The TARDIS can also mis-translate text in a given location to send a message (*fig 8.05*).

TIME LORD CUBES

Fig 8.06

Beyond the TARDIS there are other methods that can be used to carry telepathic messages. Time Lords can construct cubes, formed of six square pieces (fig 8.06), that can be used to collect their thoughts and then be projected through time and space.

These are mainly used as a Time Lord emergency messaging system. Should the cubes be unable to find Gallifrey, however, they will go unanswered and will attempt to find the nearest TARDIS for help.

DATA RETRIEVAL

Fig 8.04

Fig 8.05

Fig 8.07

Fig 8.04. Text translated from Latin.

Fig 8.05. The translation systems sending a desperate message.

Fig 8.06. Time Lord communication cube.

Fig 8.07. A new tactile interface with the telepathic circuits.

THE IDRIS INCIDENT

TELEPATHIC CIRCUIT MEMORY NODE RETRIEVAL
NODE: 7/33:04
SPATIAL CO-ORDINATES: Rift outside the known universe.
TEMPORAL CO-ORDINATES: Local Dateline: Unknown.
TARDIS CREW: The Eleventh Doctor (Gallifreyan), Amy Pond (Terran),
Rory Williams (Terran).

This node is presented as a warning if any TARDIS operators should encounter the non-corporeal entity known as 'House'.

Using emergency message cubes as lures, House had systematically tricked Gallifreyan time travellers into a trans-dimensional pocket universe, where it consumed the Artron energy of living TARDISes and killed the occupants. Several well-known Time Lords from Gallifreyan history were amongst the victims. (Detailed descriptions of these events are described in 'The Life and History of the Corsair' written by Co-ordinator Engin.)

In order to avoid the catastrophic side effects of removing a living TARDIS consciousness from the operational matrix, House used telepathic transfer technology to implant those matrixes within the bodies of humanoid victims, whose bodies had been extended past their allotted span by means of spare part surgery. It is believed that most of the Gallifreyan victims of House met their demise in this manner: used as unwilling organ donors.

This TARDIS's matrix was transplanted into the body of a young woman called Idris, allowing the ship to enter into direct verbal communication with the Doctor for the first time.

(Note: Whilst it has long been believed that the Doctor stole his capsule, conversations between the Doctor and Idris indicate that the TARDIS was not only complicit in the action, but in fact chose to run away with *him*. This information needs verification as it may well have bearing with regard to files relating to the Doctor's criminal record.)

Having removed the TARDIS matrix, House inserted itself into the TARDIS operational mainframe, taking control of all environmental, architectural and navigation systems with the aim of escaping from the bubble universe and plundering the Artron energy of this universe.

Because he was able to utilise the latent abilities of the TARDIS matrix, even whilst it was contained within its humanoid form, the Doctor successfully constructed a working control column from the wrecked remains of the numerous capsules destroyed by House, channelling Rift energy via the Idris/TARDIS symbiote and powering it to the extent that dematerialisation and travel was possible.

(Note: Attempting trans-dimensional flight using a console without the protection of the outer plasmic shell is *extremely* dangerous. It is believed that the Doctor only managed to survive this attempt because of the strong telepathic bond that he has established with the matrix of this TARDIS. Travel in this manner should

not be attempted by other Gallifreyans under any circumstances.)

Using a telepathic link to the psyche of Amy Pond as a directional indicator, the Doctor was able to pilot the scavenged console directly into a TARDIS console room.

Tricking House into transferring the body containing the TARDIS matrix back into the primary console room, the matrix was able to 'consume' House, effectively purging it from the TARDIS operational systems in order to regain control of the capsule.

Whilst it seems entirely possible that this transfer of a living TARDIS consciousness into a viable organic shell was accomplished many times by House, this TARDIS appears to be the only capsule in existence that has actually survived the process, and as a result has gained an understanding of the concept of being 'alive'. The fact that it had also been able to experience direct physical interaction with its operator gives the Doctor a unique telepathic bond with this TARDIS matrix; if possible further investigation should take place in order to capitalise on the advantages that such a close working relationship can bring.

Whilst the apparent destruction of House has likely negated any danger to other Gallifreyan time travellers within the Doctor's relative timeline TARDIS operators are warned to be wary of any temporal distress signals that might be detected within the vortex, as House obviously has an understanding of temporal mechanics and a danger is still posed by messages emanating from early portions of the timestream.

If TARDIS operators receive an emergency message cube from a Time Lord believed to be missing, please contact traffic control who will advise as to the individual's actual temporal status.

SUB-NODE RETRIEVAL
NODE: DDD/89
SPATIAL CO-ORDINATES: Earth (Terra).
TEMPORAL CO-ORDINATES: Local Dateline: 20th Century
TARDIS CREW: The Third Doctor (Gallifreyan), Elizabeth Shaw (Terran).

NOTES:

The Doctor has had previous experience of travelling through the time vortex unprotected by the outer plasmic shell during his exile on planet Earth (see CIA Files. Reference: Malfeasance Tribunal Order dated three zero nine nine zero six).

Attempting to bypass the blocks that the High Council had put upon his memory with regard to dematerialisation theory, the Doctor removed the central console from this capsule and, using energy from a primitive nuclear reactor to provide power to the controls, unexpectedly materialised in an alternate timeline running parallel to that of Twentieth-Century Earth.

Once again, it is suspected that the Doctor was only able to survive this journey because of the strong telepathic bond that he had established with the matrix of this capsule.

(NB: Removal of the central console from the control room and attempting to use alternative energy sources in order to power the controls will invalidate the warranty and could cause irreversible damage to TARDIS systems.)

THE ORSON PINK INCIDENT

TELEPATHIC CIRCUIT MEMORY NODE RETRIEVAL
NODE: 8/34:04
SPATIAL CO-ORDINATES: Earth (Terra).
TEMPORAL CO-ORDINATES: Local Dateline: 21st Century.
TARDIS CREW: The Twelfth Doctor (Gallifreyan), Clara Oswald (Terran).

Although not recommended as usual operating procedure, the TARDIS telepathic circuits can be used to extrapolate a flight path along the timeline of an individual from the moment of their birth to the moment of their death. This function can only be used if the subject to be extrapolated makes direct contact with the telepathic circuits via the interface on the console. (Note: Individuals should be advised that lapses of concentration might result in undesired mental images being projected directly to the view screens.)

The Doctor utilised this facility in order to test a hypothesis about the existence of an omnipresent universal entity using Clara Oswald as his test subject.

Because of a mental distraction at the point of operation, the TARDIS actually locked onto the timeline of Danny Pink – an associate of Miss Oswald's with whom she was attempting to start a romantic relationship.

Not realising the connection between the two of them, the Doctor then extrapolated the timelines still further, following Mr Pink's timeline to a (possibly anomalous) descendant – Orson Pink, a test pilot for one of the first Terran time travel experiments. (For further information see 'A Technological Dead-end: Magnus Greel, Zigma Technology and Early Terran Temporal Experimentation' by Cardinal Borusa.)

Ultimately the Doctor's hypothesis cannot be verified, because although there does appear to be physical evidence of an entity directly affecting its environment, no such creature can be confirmed by on-board TARDIS systems.

THE NETHERSPHERE INCIDENT

TELEPATHIC CIRCUIT MEMORY NODE RETRIEVAL
NODE: 34/8:11
SPATIAL CO-ORDINATES: Earth (Terra)
TEMPORAL CO-ORDINATES: Local Dateline: 21st Century
TARDIS CREW: The Twelfth Doctor (Gallifreyan), Clara Oswald (Terran).

NOTES:

The TARDIS telepathic circuits constantly monitor TARDIS crewmembers once they have left the ship, both in order to augment real-time data gathering, and to assist with local language interpretation. As a result they are one of the most power-heavy systems on board, with an almost infinite range.

Whilst that power is generally harmless to the population of any planet on which a TARDIS lands, this node illustrates the dangers if that power is misused.

Encountering a newly regenerated version of the Master on the planet Earth (see CIA File: Missy), the Doctor discovered that she had harnessed the power of the TARDIS's telepathic circuit in order to 'harvest' the consciousness of the recently dead, uploading that mental pattern to the Nethersphere — an adapted form of a Gallifreyan matrix data slice.

Creating a mental environment within the data slice, Missy kept the stolen minds alive and functioning, before deleting all emotional responses and downloading those minds to empty Cyberman shells constructed by use of 'Cyber-pollen'. Every tiny particle of a 'Cyber-pollen' contained the plans to make another Cyberman. All it had to do was to make a contact with compatible living organic matter.

By distributing that pollen across the graveyards of the world, Missy was able to create a Cyber army, only ultimately defeated because of an individual — Danny Pink — who did not delete emotion from his mental makeup.

As well as abusing the telepathic systems of her TARDIS, Missy also used her dimensional matrix to fold space within the Terran structure known as St Paul's Cathedral to create a dimensionally transcendental area in which she could hide the first soldiers of her Cyber army.

INVALIDATING THE WARRANTY

Under no circumstances should a TARDIS be permitted to travel outside the perimeter of Gallifrey's transduction barriers unless it is certified to be flightworthy. Operating a TARDIS that is in drastic need of repair will almost certainly result in situations that endanger the lives of the crew and the structural integrity of the ship itself.

This TARDIS exhibited a range of functional irregularities when, early on, it was taken from the repair bay without authorisation. Throughout the centuries, there have been significant instances where the negligence of its operator has violated the terms of use of this craft.

The door-locking mechanism is constructed in such a way to secure the ship during flight. Tampering with this system may result in the exterior doors opening during materialisation which can result is some serious dimensional issues (see Section X – Troubleshooting). You also risk being sucked out into the space-time vortex (fig 9.01).

MAINTENANCE

There are many other vital systems that require regular maintenance. The fluid links, for example, should be routinely checked. Failure to do so may make an emergency dematerialisation (fig 9.02) problematic and can result in

DATA RETRIEVAL

Fig 9.01

Fig 9.02

toxic mercury vapour contaminating the craft.

If the environmental systems are neglected, you may find yourself in a situation where the automatic oxygen generation system, that provides a breathable atmosphere throughout the ship's almost boundless interior, proves unreliable. In these situations the TARDIS can still maintain a viable atmosphere by recycling air from outside the ship, and using an emergency supply of oxygen stored in cylinders (fig. 9.03). If, however, the TARDIS is submerged or deposits on its outer shell build up to form an airtight crust (fig 9.04), anyone still on board is in danger of being asphyxiated.

Fig 9.01. The dangers of the doors being open during take-off.

Fig 9.02. An emergency dematerialisation.

Fig 9.03. Oxygen levels low.

Fig 9.04. The TARDIS is smothered.

Fig 9.05

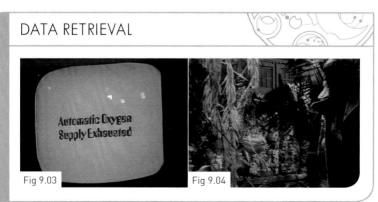

Automatic Oxygen
Supply Exhausted

Fig 9.03

Fig 9.04

Fig 9.05. An exploded
image of the TARDIS.

Fig 9.06

Fig 9.07

There are many actions that will put undue strain on the TARDIS infrastructure. Possibly the most dangerous manoeuvre a TARDIS can perform is a time ram – where a materialisation is attempted in the exact same point in space and time as another planet or craft.

Although the force generators tap into vast power reserves, using them against formidable entities or massive stellar bodies (see page 104: Section VII – Force Fields: Case Studies) will cause

system-wide damage.

If both your force field and materialisation circuit go offline, one way to counter any extreme gravitational forces is to cause the TARDIS to spin like a ball, which should redirect the energy of any impact into deflecting your vessel away from the influence of the gravity whirlpool.

To some extent, the TARDIS is able to weather these kind of extreme situations. If the TARDIS exceeds its own time parameters, by drifting into the distant future, it is in a much more vulnerable position (see p124: Case Studies).

Fortunately there are few races that can cause damage to the TARDIS under optimum operating conditions. Only the Daleks, at the height of their powers, were capable of inflicting any serious harm. Some factions have developed chronon loop technology – which

Fig 9.06. The Doctor takes the TARDIS to the end of his – and its – own timestream.

Fig 9.07. The TARDIS defenses are attacked by Z-neutrino energy.

can be used to encircle a TARDIS and disable its defences. Should this happen, they can then bombard the outer shell with Z-neutrino energy, destroying the ship entirely (fig 9.07).

UPGRADES

Most TARDISes were significantly upgraded with the necessary modifications to engage in battle during the Time War and, after that point, they were much better equipped. Subsequently, even in cases where the shields are not configured and a collision results in another vessel breaking through into the control room, the architectural configuration

systems can quickly repair the damage. A concerted effort to corrupt the systems, however, can still result in an apocalyptic explosion (see p126: Case Studies).

At the end of the TARDIS's functional lifespan it will be decommissioned and repurposed. It is forbidden to attempt to pilot an earlier version of the TARDIS to this space-time event. It is not merely in breach of the terms of this TARDIS's warranty – it contravenes the Laws of Time. One place you must never go when you're a time traveller is to the end of your own personal timeline, and the TARDIS will reject any attempt to take it to this final destination (fig 9.06).

DATA RETRIEVAL

Fig 9.08

Being a source of such awesome power the TARDIS can also be a danger to itself and the world around it. The link to the Eye of Harmony must never be opened. It will instantly begin to have an adverse effect on the molecular structure of any nearby matter — at first in subtle ways (fig 9.08), and then catastrophically. Any nearby planet will be pulled inside out. (See page 38: Section IV — The TARDIS Engines: Case Studies).

Fig 9.08. The power of the Eye of Harmony distorting the world around it.

THE FRONTIOS INCIDENT

TELEPATHIC CIRCUIT MEMORY NODE RETRIEVAL
NODE: 6N/91
SPATIAL CO-ORDINATES: Frontios, Veruna System.
TEMPORAL CO-ORDINATES: Boundary Error – Time Parameters Exceeded.
TARDIS CREW: The Fifth Doctor (Gallifreyan), Tegan Jovanka (Terran),
Vislor Turlough (Trion).

This node is presented as an example of why special care must been taken when operating a Time Capsule at the limit of its temporal reach.

A combination of circumstances arose on the planet Frontios where the TARDIS materialised within the influence of a psycho-organic gravitational field, generated by a segmented arthropod species of the genus *Phenomenoptera*, (See Index File: Tractators). The magnitude of this gravitational field, coupled with unexpected systems failures in essential TARDIS instrumentation caused by the Boundary Error, resulted in a malfunction to the Hostile Action Displacement System.

Shortly after materialisation this TARDIS was caught up in an artificially instigated meteor bombardment of the planet's surface, and therefore the HADS system engaged. However, instead of relocating the capsule to a safe location, the outer plasmic shell was breached and a large proportion of the craft's interior dimensions reallocated underground, spatially redistributed to optimise the packing efficiency of the real-time envelope.

Meanwhile, the Doctor, Tegan and Turlough became engaged with one of the last surviving colonies of the human race, which had been fleeing the imminent destruction of the planet Earth when they were forced down on Frontios.

(Note: The Doctor's action here is in direct contravention to Gallifreyan laws of non-intervention and is currently being reviewed by a judicial board. For further information see CIA Files, case number 262704K.)

Re-integration of the capsule geometry was only possible due to the intervention of the Gravis – swarm leader of the Tractators – by means of the creature's psycho-organic gravitational attraction.

Whilst the specific combination of circumstances that causes this malfunction are extremely rare, capsule operators should nonetheless ensure that any non-vital automated systems are set to 'safe mode' before materialisation in the event of time parameters being exceeded.

THE TOTAL EVENT COLLAPSE INCIDENT

TELEPATHIC CIRCUIT MEMORY NODE RETRIEVAL
NODE: 5/31:13
SPATIAL CO-ORDINATES: Earth (Terra)
TEMPORAL CO-ORDINATES: Local dateline: 21st Century.
TARDIS CREW: The Eleventh Doctor (Gallifreyan), Amy Pond (Terran),
Rory Williams (Terran), River Song (species information restricted by CIA).

All time travel is theoretically dangerous, but operators should be aware that in extreme circumstances the destruction of a TARDIS whilst in time travel mode could result in a Total Event Collapse, effectively causing the destruction of all matter both spatially and temporally.

This is known to have occurred at least once when the Kovarian Faction of the Silence, in an attempt to stop the Doctor setting in motion a series of events that would result in him reaching the planet Trenzalore (see Section XI, Node 33/7:13) sabotaged the Doctor's TARDIS, causing it to explode whilst travelling in the Time Vortex. This started a catastrophic cascade of destruction that ultimately wiped out every planet in existence with the exception of the planet Earth, which survived only because the burning TARDIS became a substitute sun, providing enough light and heat to keep the planet alive.

At the moment of its destruction the TARDIS was being piloted by River Song. On-board emergency protocols sealed off the control room and put her into a time loop in order to save her life. The Doctor was later able to breach that time loop in order to rescue her.

Ultimately the Doctor was successful in undoing the effects of the Total Event Collapse by using the restoration field of a temporal prison device known as the Pandorica to extrapolate the entire universe from a few billion atoms preserved from the explosion. (See Index File: the Second Big Bang.)

CASE STUDY

THE MAGNO-GRAB INCIDENT

TELEPATHIC CIRCUIT MEMORY NODE RETRIEVAL
NODE: 07/33:10
SPATIAL CO-ORDINATES: Unknown**.
TEMPORAL CO-ORDINATES: Unknown**.
TARDIS CREW: Twelfth Doctor (Gallifreyan), Clara Oswald (Terran).

NOTES:

In order to better acquaint Clara Oswald with the operations of TARDIS systems, the Doctor set all operating systems to basic mode. (**NB: This action suspended real-time data gathering, thus there is no space / time data for this event.)

Whilst in this mode the TARDIS was snared by the magnetic traction beam of a salvage spacecraft, causing severe damage to all systems. (Magno-grabs are an illegal traction system outlawed in most galaxies, due to their ability to disable whole vessels not fitted with shield oscillators. The TARDIS shield oscillators are automatically disengaged when the flight controls are set to basic mode.)

Once on-board the salvage ship, the TARDIS suffered multiple catastrophic systems malfunctions. Widespread venting of fuel/coolant and an explosion within the engine room necessitated activation of full emergency procedures. Primary systems concentrated on limiting damage caused by the explosion of the main engine by generating a temporal stasis lock around the engine room and ensuring crew safety. Whilst the Doctor was successfully ejected through the outer plasmic shell, Clara became trapped within the failing TARDIS systems and hunted by future echoes of herself — an event caused by the explosion of the TARDIS engines.

The ship therefore created 'safe zones' by generating echoes of the console room, temporally stable sub-dimensions within the TARDIS shell that could be used as refuges (see Index File: State of Temporal Grace).

In normal circumstances this level of damage would be enough to render a TARDIS permanently non-operable; however, temporal rifts caused by the damage allowed the Doctor to reset the timelines by making an unauthorised crossing of his own timeline.

TARDIS operators are reminded that on no account should the capsule be set to basic mode without first ensuring that the immediate area is clear, and that persistent crossing and re-crossing of one's own timeline is PROHIBITED.

TROUBLESHOOTING

The TARDIS is not simply a machine. It is a complex ecosystem that develops over time. If it refuses to take you where you want to go, or deposits you in inconvenient situations – it may be an expression of the TARDIS's greater understanding of its own place within the fabric of time.

There are numerous ways in which the TARDIS can malfunction, but it is always worth considering if any anomalous behaviour is deliberate – that the TARDIS knows what needs to happen. Below is a list of problems you may encounter when operating this craft.

PROBLEM: The fault locator (*fig 10.01*) registers errors in every system. The doors, scanner, control console and members of the crew start behaving in an unusual fashion.

EXPLANATION/SOLUTION: The TARDIS systems are cryptically communicating a situation of extreme peril. You should check the fast return switch (*fig 10.02*) hasn't jammed. If this button isn't released it will send the TARDIS hurtling back to the celestial origins of your chosen destination, where hostile conditions may exceed the vessel's tolerance levels.

Fig 10.01. The fault locator.

Fig 10.02. The fast-return switch.

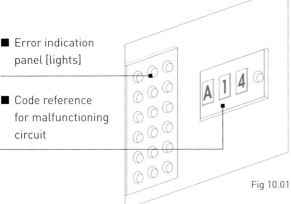

- Error indication panel [lights]

- Code reference for malfunctioning circuit

A 1 4

Fig 10.01

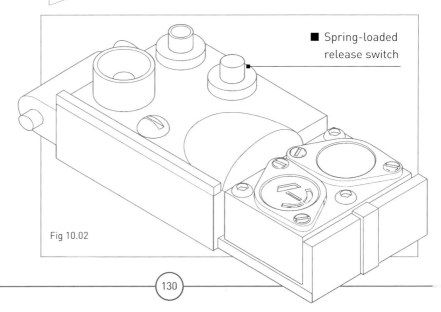

- Spring-loaded release switch

Fig 10.02

Rather than initiating emergency evasive procedures, the TARDIS may use this scenario to encourage a better working relationship between the crew, offering them clues to solve and an opportunity to evaluate their reaction to each other.

PROBLEM: The TARDIS appears to have landed on a planet of giants (fig 10.03).
EXPLANATION/SOLUTION: An overload in the dimension control circuits, caused by the exterior doors opening during materialisation, has reduced the crew considerably in size. This state of affairs can be reversed by repeating the same sequence of events that occurred during landing, when taking off.

PROBLEM: Various temporal anomalies are observed. Exiting the ship, crewmembers discover they are unable to interact with objects or other people.
EXPLANATION/SOLUTION: The TARDIS jumped a time track when it materialised. There should only be a short delay before normality is restored. This is a very rare phenomenon, but it will afford the crew a glimpse into the future – possibly allowing them to avert an imminent disaster when they arrive back in their own dimension.

PROBLEM: Unintentionally, the TARDIS rematerialises in the same location.
EXPLANATION/SOLUTION: Although it will have no effect on the craft's ability to travel in time, a fault in the gravitational bearings can result in the TARDIS being unable to break away from any large mass. Upon rematerialising,

the TARDIS will have tracked the spatial location over time, of any planet or spacecraft it took off from and will return to the same spot.

PROBLEM: The outside of the TARDIS is invisible.
EXPLANATION/SOLUTION: There is a fault in the visual stabliser circuit. It should be noted that if an attempt is made to patch the circuit with simple alien technology, it can only be a matter of time before it fails again.

PROBLEM: The console unit randomly sends people standing nearby into the past or future.
EXPLANATION/SOLUTION: The console can generate temporal fields that displace personnel in time – usually only a few seconds, but in some instances it can briefly project people days into their own past, like ghosts from the future (fig 10.04).

DATA RETRIEVAL

Fig 10.03

Fig 10.04

Fig 10.03. A shrunken TARDIS following a compromised materialisation.

Fig 10.04. Ghosts from the future.

PROBLEM: The external scanner isn't working

EXPLANATION/SOLUTION: This is likely to be the result of a fault in the interstitial beam synthesiser. Fortunately, this component is easily repaired.

PROBLEM: There is a loss of power on all systems.

EXPLANATION/SOLUTION: There are relatively few external forces that can drain power from the TARDIS. One destination that should be avoided is Exxilon – a planet which was once home to the supreme beings of the universe. The city they built is capable of draining any power source on the planet.

PROBLEM: It appears that the TARDIS is trapped inside itself.

EXPLANATION/SOLUTION: One possibility is a gravity bubble (see page 134: Case Study), but there are other things that can cause this kind of dimensional anomaly – such as executing an emergency materialisation when leaving conceptual space.

PROBLEM: The TARDIS outer shell begins to shrink – and the doors haven't opened during materialisation.

EXPLANATION/SOLUTION: First, check that the TARDIS has not materialised within the compression field of a Miniscope – a device that stores miniaturised versions of creatures that can be displayed on a screen to entertain others.

If this isn't the issue, it may be that an attempt to repair the TARDIS using block transfer computation has caused dimensional issues (see page 134: Case Study).

Alternatively, it may be a symptom of dimensional leeching, triggered by an alternative reality with different physical laws breaking through into our own (see page 136: Case Study).

PROBLEM: Crewmembers either age rapidly, or regress to childhood, as the TARDIS travels through time (*fig 10.05a* and *10.05b*).

EXPLANATION/SOLUTION: The travellers have become infected with a mutated viral strain associated with unethical experiments in Time Lord biology. With a suitable power source, a metamorphic symbiosis regenerator can cure this condition.

PROBLEM: The engines have stalled.

EXPLANATION/SOLUTION: The ship is running low on transitional elements which need to be replenished

Fig 10.05a and *10.05b.* Escaping from a warp ellipse unexpectedly affects the age of the Doctor's companions Nyssa and Tegan.

DATA RETRIEVAL

Fig 10.05a

Fig 10.05b

Fig 10.06

(see page 69: The Console – Controls & Functions: Power).

PROBLEM: The TARDIS suddenly dematerialises of its own accord and refuses to be piloted.
EXPLANATION/SOLUTION: If you've ruled out an emergency materialisation triggered by the HADS (see page 81) then there are a number of other explanations.

If the TARDIS detects a temporal anomaly it will take immediate evasive measures. Owing to their paradoxical nature, some of these anomalies may result in the TARDIS actually causing the problem it seeks to avoid.

Another potential cause may be local time distortion, which can trigger a materialisation loop. You can try to nullify the disturbance using the zig-zag plotter (fig 10.06).

In very rare circumstances, an unexplained glitch may cause the TARDIS

to temporarily abandon members of its crew. Non-qualified personnel should seek advice from any Time Lords who can help.

PROBLEM: The TARDIS refuses to land – any attempt to materialise results an overload in the navigational systems.
EXPLANATION/SOLUTION: Temporal distortions can make it impossible to land in certain locations. The local disruption can be neutralised by using a time distortion equaliser that uses an intuitive gemstone as its 'onboard computer'.

PROBLEM: The TARDIS internal dimensions are isolated from the outer shell. The exterior resembles a small box.
EXPLANATION/SOLUTION: The TARDIS has activated siege mode (see page 136: Case Study).

Fig 10.06. Local time distortion traps the TARDIS in a materialisation loop.

THE LOGOPOLIS INCIDENT

TELEPATHIC CIRCUIT MEMORY NODE RETRIEVAL
NODE: 5V/41
SPATIAL CO-ORDINATES: Earth (Terra).
TEMPORAL CO-ORDINATES: Local Dateline: 20th Century
TARDIS CREW: The Fourth Doctor (Gallifreyan), Adric (Alzarian).

NOTES:

Intending to use the Logopolitan science of Block Transfer Computation to rectify a fault in the chameleon circuit, the Doctor materialised this TARDIS around an actual Terran police box in order to obtain the precise mathematical measurements of that object necessary for the procedure.

Unbeknownst to him, however, the Master had already materialised his own capsule in the same location and the resulting dimensional anomaly resulted in a dangerously powerful gravity bubble and a recursive spatial repetition.

Having successfully escaped from that gravity bubble (see Case Studies; Section VI – Corridors of Eternity, page 101) the Doctor's subsequent visit to Logopolis itself caused further problems when the Logopolitan computations resulted in a mathematical error that caused the outer plasmic shell to shrink.

By using sonic projectors to create a zone of temporary stasis around the TARDIS, the Monitor of Logopolis had time to locate and rectify the error in the computations (caused by the Master's external interference) before the internal dimensions were terminally disrupted, and was able to stabilise the dimensional anomaly.

TARDIS operators are reminded that materialising one TARDIS inside another will inevitably cause complex dimensional anomalies that are not always possible to rectify. Please refer to standing instructions if in any doubt.

THE TWO-DIMENSIONAL CROSSOVER INCIDENT

TELEPATHIC CIRCUIT MEMORY NODE RETRIEVAL
NODE: 8/34:9
SPATIAL CO-ORDINATES: Earth (Terra).
TEMPORAL CO-ORDINATES: Local Dateline: 21st Century
TARDIS CREW: The Twelfth Doctor (Gallifreyan), Clara Oswald (Terran).

NOTES:

Whereas the existence of two- and one-dimensional universes has long been postulated, proof of their existence was only confirmed during an encounter by the Doctor on the planet Earth during his twelfth incarnation.

Beings from a two-dimensional universe making what appears to be a fact finding mission into our universe (See Index File: The Boneless), were able to drain dimensional energy from the TARDIS, causing the exterior plasmic shell to shrink. TARDIS failsafe systems prevented a similar reduction of the interior space; however the resulting dimensional anomaly resulted in the Doctor being unable to exit the TARDIS due to the shrinking of the exterior doorway. (Note: operators should be aware that should this happen, and the effects are not reversible, then there is currently no documented way of exiting from the TARDIS interior.)

With systems failing, the Doctor became aware that the TARDIS was vulnerable in its diminutive state. To avoid destruction beneath the wheels of a Terran rail vehicle, the Doctor activated the siege mode protocols.

Siege mode effectively sets the TARDIS into a state of temporal stasis, whereby nothing can get in or out. It also defaults the look of the outer plasmic shell to factory basic.

THE TIMELINE ERROR INCIDENT

TELEPATHIC CIRCUIT MEMORY NODE RETRIEVAL
NODE: 36/10:X
SPATIAL CO-ORDINATES: Earth.
TEMPORAL CO-ORDINATES: Local Dateline: 20th Century.
TARDIS CREW: The Twelfth Doctor (Gallifreyan), The First Doctor. (Gallifreyan), Captain Archibald Hamish Lethbridge-Stewart (Terran).

NOTES:

Whilst the rules prohibiting Time Lords crossing their own personal timelines and interacting with previous incarnations of themselves are generally imposed because of the temporal anomalies that can occur (and under NO circumstances should operators attempt to emulate the Doctor's persistent flouting of the law in this regard), there are occasions where the consequences of these actions can be more wide-reaching.

During the events just prior to his looming regeneration, the Twelfth Doctor landed this TARDIS in the exact space/time location where his first incarnation had landed, at the South Pole of the planet Earth during the first Cyberman invasion (see Index File: The Destruction of Mondas).

Because both incarnations of the Doctor were attempting to hold back their regenerations at the time, both of them had the potential to die at exactly the same moment in history, creating an impossibly complex temporal paradox. Whilst the space/time continuum tried to make sense of the anomaly, a 'timeline error' occurred, effectively freezing all of planet Earth in a single moment whilst still allowing both incarnations of the Doctor freedom of movement.

At the same time that the timeline error occurred, a time-travelling species called the Testimony were attempting to lift a captain from

the planet's First World War from his timestream. (Index File information relating to the Testimony is currently barred pending a decision on official Gallifreyan policy; put briefly, the Testimony travel the space/time continuum, lifting the human near-dead momentarily from their timestreams, duplicating their memories, and then returning the humans to the moment of their dissolution without any recall of the process. Although there are temporal and legal ramifications to these actions, the resource that the Testimony have created is a significant one, and because of this the High Council of Time Lords is currently debating whether to enter into negotiations with them in order to merge information that they hold with the Gallifreyan memory banks currently held within the Matrix.)

The 'timeline error' was eventually rectified by both incarnations of the Doctor accepting the inevitability of their regenerations and setting their own personal timeline back on track. It must be noted, however, that the Doctor *did* interfere

in the timeline of Captain Archibald Hamish Lethbridge-Stewart by not actually returning him to the moment of his death, but instead to a moment a few hours later. Whilst the Doctor justified this action as being just one less dead body on a battlefield, the survival of Captain Lethbridge-Stewart, and the subsequent lineage that resulted from his survival, has a significant impact on the events that occur on Earth from this point on.

WARNING NOTE:
REGENERATION INSIDE A TARDIS
Whilst both incarnations of the Doctor regenerated inside their capsules at the conclusion of this event, only the Twelfth Doctor's regeneration caused severe damage to TARDIS systems, and this has led to an investigation by

the Black Hole Shipyards as to why this might have occurred.

The conclusion of the report is that whilst regeneration early in a Time Lord's lifecycle appears to have no adverse effect, regenerations that occur later in life — particularly if those regenerations take place within the console room of a Type 40 TT Capsule — have a direct physical impact because of psychic feedback through the telepathic circuits.

Whilst the Doctor's first regeneration had a negligible effect on TARDIS systems, study of memory nodes has revealed there was a marked increase in energy release at the point of their fifth regeneration.

By the time of his regeneration into later bodies, this energy release was at dangerous levels and caused catastrophic damage to the

TARDIS control room, requiring a complete reset of the internal architecture and major systems updates by the auto repair circuits.

TARDIS operators in the second half of their regeneration cycles are warned that should they find themselves in a life-threatening situation that might result in bodily regeneration they should endeavour to find a safe location well away from their capsule or, if that is not possible, to ensure

that all TARDIS fire safety protocols are set to their maximum settings.

(As a result of this investigation all Time Lords in the sixth incarnation or higher who request to take a capsule off world will have to submit to a thorough medical examination by the Surgeon General. This operational procedure will take place with immediate effect to avoid unnecessary damage to TARDIS systems.)

SECTION XI

MODIFICATIONS

Fig 11.01. An entropy field destroys the universe.

Fig 11.02. The void left by a TARDIS that's been integrated with a terrestrial structure.

Fig 11.03. A Time Lord containment unit.

I t is possible for accomplished Time Lord engineers to repurpose the TARDIS systems, so that your capsule can be used for a variety of functions beyond simply traversing the space-time vortex.

Although not strictly a modification of a TARDIS, the basic principles of the TARDIS construction – creating a shell that contains vast interior dimensions – can be used to create containment units (fig 11.03). This can be useful for simple storage purposes or, in extreme cases, when Gallifrey is drawn into conflict, to incarcerate prisoners.

The most common purpose of reconfiguring established TARDIS systems is to manipulate the fabric of space and time.

Two TARDISes linked together can be used as time cone inverters. This technology is capable of applying temporal inversion isometry to sections of space-time – and should be capable of holding back an entropy field (fig 11.01) that threatens to unravel the causal nexus of the whole universe.

The TARDIS systems can also be substantially adapted so that it can sustain a temporal paradox (see page 144 – Case Studies).

DECOMMISSIONING

When TARDISes are decommissioned, their systems can be modified so that the outer plasmic shell is incorporated into the fabric of an existing building. If this is used to conceal a disused TARDIS offworld, then it's important that the TARDIS is not moved, as the resulting void will manifest itself as a blue haze (fig 11.02), potentially drawing alien attention to Time Lord activities.

Some TARDISes are ultimately used to memorialise their primary operator and can act as a kind of tomb (see page 146 – Case Studies).

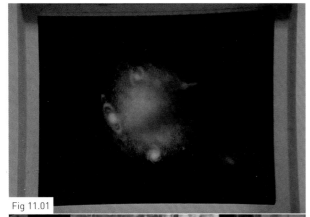

Fig 11.01

Fig 11.02

Fig 11.03

■ This unit can be re-activated by coming into contact with an Artron signature (see page 14)

■ Re-named the Genesis Ark by the Daleks

■ Bigger on the inside

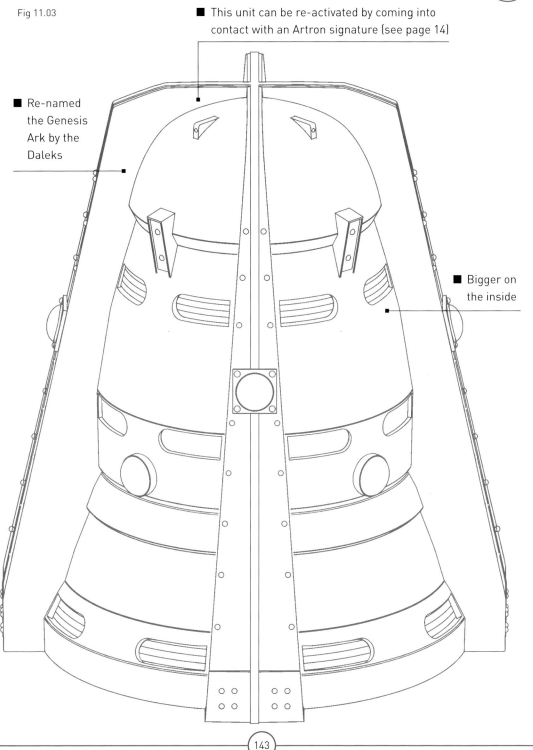

THE PARADOX MACHINE INCIDENT

The Case Studies contained in this chapter refer to extreme space/time events that simply would not have been allowed to happen if Gallifrey and the High Council of Time Lords had not been taken out of Time at the climax of the Great Time War. (see Celestial Intervention Files. Reference: The War Doctor).

Whilst it is unlikely that TARDIS operators will ever encounter scenarios as extreme as those annotated below, they are presented as a warning of the dangerous consequences that can occur if the Laws of Time are not adhered to.

TELEPATHIC CIRCUIT MEMORY NODE RETRIEVAL
NODE: 3/29:13
SPATIAL CO-ORDINATES: Utopia / Earth (Terra).
TEMPORAL CO-ORDINATES: Local Dateline: The Far End of Time / 21st Century.
TARDIS CREW: The Tenth Doctor (Gallifreyan), Martha Jones (Terran), Captain Jack Harkness (Terran).

Reacting to contact with the immortal time agent known as Captain Jack Harkness (see Index Files: The Face of Boe/Torchwood) the TARDIS travelled forward to the far end of time, and the far end of the universe, to the distant planet of Utopia. Here the Doctor encountered the Master, who had gone into hiding following the events of the Great Time War after using a Chameleon Arch, which obscured his physiognomy and personality even from himself (See CIA Files: The War Master).

Interaction with the Doctor triggered memories supressed by the Chameleon Arch and the Master regained access to his original personality. Mortally injured, the Master stole this TARDIS from the Doctor and piloted it to Twenty-first Century Earth where he modified the central console in order to create a Paradox Machine.

The Master then used this Paradox Machine to stabilise an alternate timeline where an

aggressive warmongering species known as the Toclafane (in fact the ultimate form of *Homo sapiens*) could return through time and conquer their planet of origin with the aim of creating a vast militaristic empire.

Imprisoned by the Master, and forced into extreme old age without regeneration, the Doctor almost failed to stop this dangerous alteration to the space/time continuum. Ultimately it was his associates Martha Jones and Jack Harkness who enabled his escape from the Master, and Jack's subsequent destruction of the Paradox Machine that allowed the timelines to reset to their correct pattern.

THE 'DEATH OF THE DOCTOR' INCIDENT

TELEPATHIC CIRCUIT MEMORY NODE RETRIEVAL
NODE: 33/7:13
SPATIAL CO-ORDINATES: Trenzalore
TEMPORAL CO-ORDINATES: Local Dateline: Unknown.
TARDIS CREW: The Eleventh Doctor (Gallifreyan), Clara Oswald (Terran).

Tricked by an alien entity known as the Great Intelligence, the Doctor was forced into travelling to the very end of his own personal timestream, to the planet Trenzalore — the site of his death and subsequent entombment.

By planting the space/time co-ordinates of that event inside the mind of a primitive from Nineteenth Century Earth, and revealing those co-ordinates to the Doctor's friends in that time zone (See Index File: The Paternoster Gang), the Doctor was ultimately able to extrapolate

a workable route through the vortex from the mind of his associate Clara Oswald, breaking the First Law of Time and accessing the final moments of his own timestream.

Because of the complex time anomaly that surrounds Trenzalore — a time paradox where the Doctor both lives and dies (Restricted CIA Files: The Doctor — Second Regeneration Cycle) — the matrix of this capsule initially resisted the Doctor in his attempts to reach that planet, shutting down essential systems and locking the ship in orbit in the

hope of restricting the Doctor's interaction with the anomaly.

Reckless action on the Doctor's part resulted in all capsule antigravity systems being shut down, and the TARDIS falling to the planet's surface with enough force that the outer plasmic shell was actually damaged.

(NB: TARDIS operators are reminded that any deliberate damage caused to capsules whilst under their control negates all warranties and that costs and duties for repairs will be charged to the appropriate colleges. A full breakdown of costs and relative timescales for maintenance and repair schedules can be obtained from the matrix of the Gallifreyan Black Hole Shipyards.)

Not content with merely landing on the planet, the Doctor compounded the anomaly still further by actually locating his tomb and entering it.

The tomb itself was this capsule; the death of the Doctor caused the matrix to go into grief trauma and shut down completely.

A side effect of a dying TARDIS is that the dimension dams start breaking down. This is commonly referred to as a 'size leak'. Internal dimensions start to permeate the outer plasmic shell causing the exterior to expand to enormous size.

In order to prevent any non-Gallifreyan interference with TARDIS systems after its 'death' the matrix deleted the console from the control room, replacing it with a visual representation of the Doctor's timeline, as a form of 'shrine' to his life.

The Great Intelligence utilised this 'shrine' to physically enter the Doctor's timestream, effectively deleting his actions from history. It was left to Clara Oswald to undo the actions of the Intelligence by entering the Doctor's timestream herself, directly influencing his actions during each of his incarnations in order to restore the universal timeline to its correct path.

(NB: In direct contradiction to the testimony of both the Doctor and the TARDIS matrix, Clara Oswald seems to have been instrumental in the Doctor's decision to steal this particular capsule (or the Capsule's decision to steal this particular Time Lord) from Gallifrey. However, it is entirely possible that the TARDIS had some telepathic influence over Miss Oswald at the time. Temporal investigations are ongoing.)

SUB-NODE RETRIEVAL
NODE: S/13
SPATIAL CO-ORDINATES: Trenzalore.
TEMPORAL CO-ORDINATES: Local Dateline: Unknown.
TARDIS CREW: The Eleventh Doctor (Gallifreyan), Clara Oswald (Terran).

NOTES:

With the Doctor's personal timeline back on track, it was inevitable that his travels would ultimately lead him back to Trenzalore, effectively putting into action the events that would lead to his eventual death in accordance with established history.

Summoned by the Papal Mainframe, the Doctor landed on Trenzalore to investigate a signal being broadcast throughout the universe. That signal originated from the High Council of Gallifrey, attempting communication from their time-locked planet through cracks in the universe caused by the Doctor's TARDIS exploding (See Section IX, Case Study Node 5/31:13).

Appointing himself protector of Trenzalore, the Doctor stayed on the planet to the end of his regeneration cycle, defending the planet from direct attack by those forces able to breach the perimeter set up by the Papal Mainframe.

If time had continued along its allotted path then events would ultimately have led to the Doctor's death and entombment within this capsule. However, the decision was made to grant the Doctor a second regeneration cycle, effectively negating his death within the existing timeline and creating a permanent temporal anomaly around the planet Trenzalore.

OTHER TARDISES ARE AVAILABLE

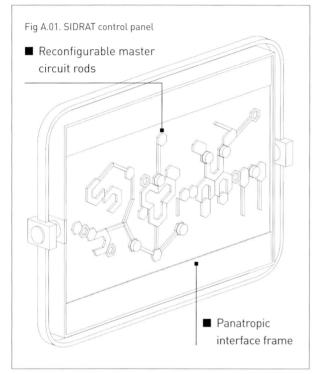

Fig A.01. SIDRAT control panel

■ Reconfigurable master circuit rods

■ Panatropic interface frame

Fig A.02

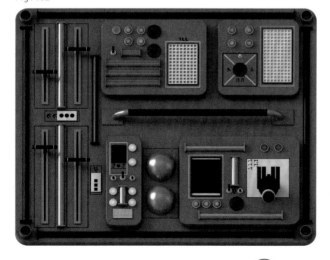

This Type 40 TARDIS is one of 305 capsules registered for operation – and the only one that hasn't been deregistered since.

It is pre-dated by many other TT capsules. Some of these are of a more primitive design – such as the SIDRATs which had a limited lifespan as a result of rudimentary dimensional flexibility circuits and hard-wired remote control capability. These capsules used a geometric control interface based on a simplified version of Gallifreyan notation (fig A.01).

Providing it is correctly maintained – and not augmented with improvised modifications – the Type 40 is a serviceable model. In recent centuries, however, the Type 40 has been superseded by newer TARDISes.

During its travels this TARDIS has been able to scan and assess the functionality of other models that it has encountered. Details follow of interesting variations from the Type 40 model (see also Unauthorised TARDIS Use entries).

TYPE 12: The Type 12 is one of the earliest TARDISes known to have survived. The dangerous Time Lord criminal Salyavin – whose mental powers have allowed him to evade the Time Lord justice system – salvaged the last Type 12 capsule before it could be dismantled. This early model predates the more familiar six-sided control console – with basic functions operated from a single panel (fig A.02).

TYPE 40 – MARK IV: The Mark IV is the updated version of the Mark III TARDIS covered in this manual. It features a number of incremental improvements. A Mark IV operated by a Time Lord known as the Monk was encountered (and sabotaged on various occasions) during the Doctor's travels.

TYPE 57: The Type 57 is recommended as a popular trade-in option for this Type 40 capsule when the operator wishes to upgrade.

Fig A.02. Type 12 control console.

Fig A.03. The Master's TARDIS.

UNAUTHORISED TARDIS USE

PRIMARY OPERATOR: THE MASTER (GALLIFREYAN).

The Master is one of the most evil and corrupt beings the Time Lord race has ever produced. His/her many incarnations have operated a number of TARDISes that they managed to acquire. They are even more inclined than the Doctor to adapt their TARDIS's systems and most of these machines have been rendered inoperable — frequently leaving them stranded.

In his encounters with the Doctor, the Master operated a TARDIS with a fully functional chameleon circuit. Even so, it would often default to certain pre-programmed patterns, such as a grandfather clock and a simple column (fig A.03).

Data collection reveals that on occasions when it crossed the path of the Doctor's, the Master's TARDIS had often adopted a similar desktop theme with subtle variations.

In her most recent incarnation, the Master — or Missy, as she became known — would often travel using a vortex manipulator; what became of the Type 45 TARDIS (see pages 152 and 153 – fig A.04) she had acquired during her previous incarnation is unknown.

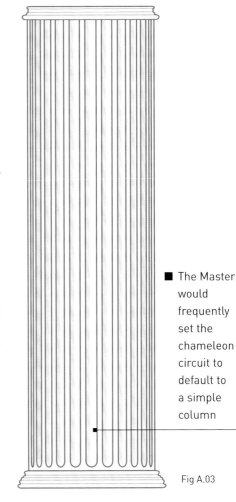

■ The Master would frequently set the chameleon circuit to default to a simple column

Fig A.03

MISSY'S TARDIS

Fig A.04. A Type 45 TARDIS appropriated by the Doctor's arch-enemy.

THE RANI'S TARDIS

Fig A.05. The Rani's control room, including some examples of her diabolical experiments.

UNAUTHORISED TARDIS USE

PRIMARY OPERATOR: THE RANI (GALLIFREYAN).
ADDITIONAL PERSONNEL: URAK (TETRAP).

The Rani is a contemporary of the Doctor — an accomplished chemist, who left Gallifrey to pursue a series of unsanctioned experiments. She also operates a TARDIS that is superior to the Doctor's, complete with a Stattenheim remote control.

Fig A.06

It has been noted that the Rani tends to subjugate natives of the planets she visits and, because of this, doesn't deem it necessary to use the chameleon circuit to camouflage her vessel, preferring to use various default patterns (fig A.07a and A.07b).

Her TARDIS includes many elaborate internal spaces designed to facilitate her experiments (fig A.06). The control space includes improvements on early capsules, including a tactile control interface and a modified circular framework version of the time column (see pages 154 and 155 — fig A.05).

Fig A.06. The interior workspace including lit roundels.

Fig A.07. Examples of the outer shell of the Rani's TARDIS.

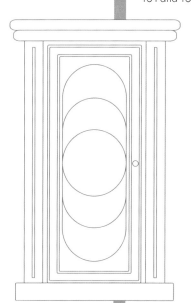

Fig A.07a

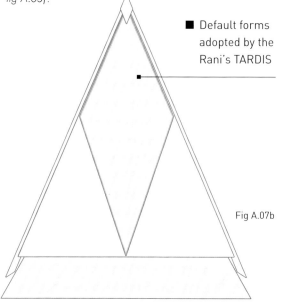

■ Default forms adopted by the Rani's TARDIS

Fig A.07b

UNAUTHORISED TARDIS USE

Fig A.08

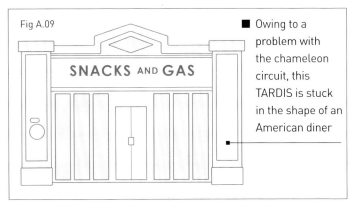

Fig A.09

SNACKS AND GAS

■ Owing to a problem with the chameleon circuit, this TARDIS is stuck in the shape of an American diner

PRIMARY OPERATOR: CLARA OSWALD (TERRAN).
ADDITIONAL PERSONNEL: ASHILDR/'ME' (GENETICALLY-AUGMENTED TERRAN).

The Type 40 with which this manual is paired is not the only TARDIS stolen by the Doctor. A further, newer model was appropriated by the Twelfth Doctor and his companion Clara. Oddly, this second TARDIS exhibited a similar fault to the first — the chameleon circuit failed and it ended up stuck in the shape of a diner (fig A.09). Clara, and an immortal human known as 'Me', travelled in the TARDIS together (fig A.08).

Fig A.08. Clara Oswald sets out on her own adventures.

Fig A.09. Clara's TARDIS.

INDEX

BBC Books, an imprint of Ebury Publishing
20 Vauxhall Bridge Road,
London SW1V 2SA

BBC Books is part of the Penguin Random House group of companies whose addresses can be found at global.penguinrandomhouse.com

Penguin
Random House
UK

Picture credits:
Doctor Who show images © BBC. Images on p104, 105 (top) © Mat Irvine; p19 (top) © Tim Overson; 20 (top), p46 (bottom) © Matt Sanders; p11, 31, 64, 156 (top) © Mike Tucker. Artwork on p61 by Lee Binding and Gavin Rymill, published by GE Fabbri in issue 60 of the Doctor Who DVD Files. Courtesy of Eaglemoss Limited.

Doctor Who is a BBC Wales production for BBC One. 'Doctor Who', 'TARDIS' and the Doctor Who logo are trademarks of the British Broadcasting Corporation and are used under the licence.

First published by BBC Books in 2018

www.penguin.co.uk

A CIP catalogue record for this book is available from the British Library

ISBN 9781785943775

Printed and bound in Turkey by Elma Basim

Penguin Random House is committed to a sustainable future for our business, our readers and our planet. This book is made from Forest Stewardship Council® certified paper.

WITH THANKS TO

Gilbert MacKenzie Trench.

Peter Brachacki, Kenneth Sharp, Barry Newbery, Mike Kelt, Malcolm Thornton, Paul Trerise, Richard Hudolin, Ed Thomas, Michael Pickwoad, Arwel Wyn Jones and all the other TARDIS designers.

David Whitaker, Anthony Coburn, Terrance Dicks, Robert Holmes, Douglas Adams, Anthony Read, Christopher H Bidmead, Russell T Davies, Steven Moffat, Chris Chibnall and everyone else who has written about the TARDIS.

And also: John Ainsworth, Graeme Allan, Lucy Ashdown, Lee Binding, Steve Cole, Paul Condon, Neil Corry, Michael Cregan, Gabby De Matteis, Albert DePetrillo, Gary Gillatt, Isabel Hayman-Brown, Clayton Hickman, Dave Ladkin, Paul Lang, Julian Northcote, Tim Overson, Rob Ritchie, Gareth Roberts, Ed Salt, Matt Sanders, Jim Sangster, Tom Spilsbury, Paul Vyse, Peter Ware and Mark Wright.